Paintings Ca

Sage Gardens Cozy Mystery Series

Cindy Bell

Copyright © 2016 Cindy Bell
All rights reserved.

All rights reserved. No part of this publication may be reproduced or transmitted in any form or by any means, electronic or mechanical, including photocopy, recording, or any information storage or retrieval system, without permission in writing from the publisher.

This is a work of fiction. The characters, incidents and locations portrayed in this book and the names herein are fictitious. Any similarity to or identification with the locations, names, characters or history of any person, product or entity is entirely coincidental and unintentional.

All trademarks and brands referred to in this book are for illustrative purposes only, are the property of their respective owners and not affiliated with this publication in any way. Any trademarks are being used without permission, and the publication of the trademark is not authorized by, associated with or sponsored by the trademark owner.

ISBN-13: 978-1539528555

ISBN-10: 1539528553

Table of Contents

Chapter One 1

Chapter Two 13

Chapter Three... 30

Chapter Four 39

Chapter Five 54

Chapter Six 67

Chapter Seven 79

Chapter Eight 96

Chapter Nine 111

Chapter Ten 121

Chapter Eleven 137

Chapter Twelve.. 149

Chapter Thirteen 160

Chapter Fourteen 173

Chapter Fifteen.. 184

Chapter Sixteen 202

Chapter Seventeen 218

Chapter Eighteen 237

Chapter Nineteen 256

More Cozy Mysteries by Cindy Bell 259

Chapter One

Jo walked out of the yoga studio and breathed in the fresh air. She felt rejuvenated just like she did after every yoga session. She started walking briskly towards her car.

"Joanne," the deep male voice startled her slightly. She turned to see a familiar face and immediately her mind flashed back as if it hadn't been several years since he held his hand out to her to help her, when he could have left her to die, or be caught by the police. He'd lost his chance at a high value painting just to make sure that she was safe.

"Bruce." He was thinner than she remembered and his shoulders hunched some. He had once been quite an intimidating man. Now he looked old. Did she look that old, too? Her cheeks flushed at the thought. Sometimes she forgot that she was in her sixties.

"What a surprise." He smiled. A few years before Bruce sent her a letter while she was in jail detailing the way he'd changed his life. He'd turned over a new leaf and wanted to thank her for being an inspiration to him. He was referring to the fact that she now led a completely different life. She used to be a cat burglar and after turning herself in she had spent time in jail. She had replied that she was happy for him, but never pursued more contact than that. She hoped that he would remain a part of her past. But there he was standing before her. "You look just like I remember."

"Oh sure." She brushed her long, black hair back over her shoulders. She smiled at him and noticed that he was standing by the door to a gallery. Was he about to rob the place? He noticed her puzzled expression.

"Oh, this is my business."

"You own a gallery?"

"I do. Why don't you come inside and have a

look?"

Jo wanted to think of an excuse not to enter the building, but she was curious. "Okay."

Bruce unlocked the door and she followed him inside. She was immediately bathed in a myriad of colors and shapes. The walls, and the floors were painted with asymmetrical circles, triangles, and squares. Paintings not only hung on the walls, but from the ceiling on long silver chains. She felt a familiar itch along the back of her neck that spread down her arms to her fingertips. There were so many valuable paintings, just there for her taking. Even though that life was behind her, the desire still bubbled up now and then. Bruce looked all around the gallery then nodded.

"Let me just get a bottle of water." He stepped through a door and disappeared. Jo took the time to admire the paintings on the wall. She'd never lost her appreciation for such beautiful pieces. It didn't matter to her if they were dark, bright, or totally abstract. The beauty she found was in the act. Someone, somewhere, decided to open up their soul and pour it onto the canvas. "Here you go."

Jo jumped as Bruce handed her a bottle of water. "Oh, thank you."

"I didn't mean to startle you."

"It's okay. I was just a little lost inside the paintings."

"I go there sometimes, too." He swept his gaze over the paintings. "It's funny, once all I saw was dollar signs, but now, I get it. I know why people pay such large amounts for something that is one of a kind."

"I thought that you were out of the burglary and fencing business." Her defenses went up at the first mention of how much the paintings might go for.

"I am, this gallery is totally legit. Trust me, it's been a struggle to keep the doors open." She nodded as she walked behind a hanging portrait.

"So business isn't good?" She asked.

"It has been better." He cleared his throat. "Actually, there is something you might be able to help me with." Jo stood there hesitantly in anticipation of what he might say. She'd put a big part of her life behind her, and it seemed to her that helping someone that was part of it, was a big risk. But he'd helped her out a few times when they were both highly sought-after thieves. One time in particular he literally saved her life. She owed him at least the respect of listening to his problem.

As her mind spun through some of the possibilities it occurred to her that he could be suckering her into a job. She was determined to remain vigilant of his intentions.

"What is it?" she asked. There was no harm in listening.

"A few of the paintings here have gone missing."

"A break-in?" She glanced around for vulnerable entry points.

"No, not exactly. That's the strange thing. It took me a while to notice that one was gone, then another. It didn't happen all at once. It's as if one or two walk out the door each week. I only do inventory once a month, or when we sell a painting, so usually it's once a month."

"Business is that bad?"

"The economy is that bad. Nobody has the extra money to buy artwork, and those that do go to galleries with a long and well-established reputation."

"How did you get involved in selling paintings?"

"Are you asking me if I stole them first?" He grinned.

"Not exactly. But it does seem like a big step to take."

"It really wasn't. I had a lot of contacts who still wanted paintings, I just took my business legit. Unfortunately, it's a lot harder to sell paintings in the traditional way."

"I imagine so." She smiled and glanced around the ceiling at the security cameras. "What about the cameras? Didn't they pick up anything?"

"I thought they would, but the thefts are happening afterhours. The cameras haven't caught anything."

"You don't leave them on overnight?"

"I do, but there are big gaps in the security footage from late at night. I don't know if perhaps the thief knows how to turn them off. But they are always on when I open up in the morning."

"What about an alarm? It hasn't been triggered?"

"No, not once. I would have been notified."

"And the police, have you gone to them?"

"Of course not."

"Why not?" She raised an eyebrow. "If your paintings are being stolen I would assume that the police would be the first call you would make."

"Right, and give them a reason to look into my past? You and I both know that paintings can easily be stolen without being caught on camera and without triggering any kind of alarm. All the police are going to do is take pictures and alert the person who I think is responsible for this."

"Oh." She paused and turned back to face him. "You already know who the thief is?"

"I don't know for sure. But I do suspect someone. If the police get involved, he'll know that I noticed the missing paintings. Maybe you could help me look into it a bit? I'll pay you."

"I don't know," Jo said hesitantly. She wanted to help him and she could use the extra cash. "I don't want to get involved in anything illegal."

"It's nothing illegal."

"I just want to know where the money is coming from." She cleared her throat.

"Ah, I see. You're worried about helping me out. I can understand that." His jaw rippled. "Somewhat. You don't trust me. Even after what I did for you?"

Jo lowered her eyes. "I know what you did for me and that's why I would want to help you. But I don't want to get involved in anything illegal, or shady. Bruce, my life is totally different now, and I like it this way. The last thing I want is to end up in prison again."

He winced at the word. "I know that. It's a terrible thing to consider. But you don't have to worry about that with me. We must have run into each other after all these years for a reason. You know how this business works, how thieves work. It would be win-win."

"Okay," Jo said hesitantly. She could look into things a bit for him. After all he wasn't asking for her help on a job, he was asking for her help in his new life.

"Thank you. I would never have told you any of this if I didn't trust you. I know that you're on the straight and narrow, which is where I want to stay."

"Tell me more about who you suspect." She opened her bottle and took a sip.

"As I said, it's been a struggle to keep the doors open lately. I think perhaps my business partner, David Right, is getting fed up with it and decided to steal some of the paintings, claim them on our insurance, and sell them on the black market."

"That's quite a scam." Her eyes narrowed "David Right?" Jo knew of a thief named David Right. In fact, she had met him once just after he entered the scene and just before she had left it.

"Yes, that David Right."

"Do you know David well?"

"I know him very well. At least I thought I did. I wouldn't have gone into business with him otherwise. But it's the only explanation that I can come up with. He has access. He knows which paintings are valuable enough to sell, but not so valuable to be noticed as missing right away. He knows how to turn the cameras on and off, how to bypass the alarm. His personal financial situation is iffy at best. I just think he's slid back into the old lifestyle. We did a few jobs together in the old days, once you were off the scene. But I thought, like me, he was on the straight and narrow now."

"Have you thought about confronting him?"

"I can't." He grimaced. "Not unless I know for sure. If I confront him and it turns out not to be true I'll have ruined a friendship, and a partnership. I'm not willing to risk that, not without some kind of proof."

"I'll see what I can find out for you. But I don't want to have any surprises, Bruce. I want to know that you're telling me the truth and not hiding anything from me."

"I'm not that person anymore, Jo. You can trust me on that." He looked into her eyes. "I need your help."

"Send me through what information you have and I'll see what I can find out. In the meantime, just try to keep your suspicions to yourself. The moment he senses that you're looking at him for this, he will shut down to the point that we won't be able to find anything."

"I can do that." He nodded and extended his hand. "I really appreciate you helping me out here, Jo."

"No problem, Bruce. It's hard to get out of the life, and into something on the up and up. It's even harder if you can't trust your partner. We'll figure this out." She gave his hand a firm shake, then turned to leave. With every step she took she wondered if she was making the right choice. If Bruce was telling the truth then it was no big deal, but if he wasn't, then he could be trying to pull her back into a way of life that she wanted nothing to do with.

Chapter Two

Later that day Jo walked from her villa towards the lake. She wanted to clear her mind and be sure that she'd made the right decision. As she walked along the water her mind drifted from the present to the past and back again. She didn't know if she wanted to bring her past into the present. She had left that life behind. There were so many differences now. The biggest difference was that she didn't have to look over her shoulder all the time. She didn't have to wonder if there was a rival, or an officer of the law sneaking up behind her. That was a luxury that she didn't ever want to lose.

"Hey Jo!" Eddy panted a little as he caught up to her. "Didn't you hear me calling you? I've been chasing you for almost ten minutes."

She turned to face him and smiled. "Sorry Eddy, I didn't. What's up?"

"Nothing much, I just want to catch up and

see how everything is. I haven't seen you for a couple of days."

"Oh, I've been busy and I just ran into an old friend. I'm helping him out with something." She shrugged.

"Anything I can help you with?" Eddy gave her a light pat on the shoulder.

"Not at the moment, but it's nice of you to offer. I'm just doing him a favor, Eddy, thank you."

"I won't keep you. Just let me know if you need anything."

"Will do, Eddy." She smiled at him then walked away. What would he think if he knew she was doing a favor for someone from her old life? He likely wouldn't approve. As she continued on her walk she found herself naturally taking the path that led to Samantha's villa. She visited her so often that it seemed strange to walk by it. She decided to drop in. When she knocked on the back door of her villa Samantha opened it.

"Jo!"

"Hi Sam."

"Do you want to come in?"

"Sure. Actually, there's something you might be able to help me with."

"Anything." Samantha held the door open for her.

"I need you to look into someone for a friend of mine. But I need to make sure that he can't figure out we've been checking up on him."

"Did you have Eddy get someone to run a background check on him?"

"No. I don't want Eddy to know much about this."

"Ah, I see." Samantha nodded and sat down at the computer. "Eddy wouldn't cause you any problems though."

"I just prefer to keep some things to myself. Is that okay? I'm not putting you in an awkward position am I?"

"No, it's fine. Trust me, I keep plenty of things from Eddy, too. He still sees things a little too black and white, though he's calmed down quite a bit I think. He's adjusting to civilian life."

"Hmm, sometimes he still thinks he has his badge and his gun."

"Well, he does have Chris." Samantha laughed as she thought about the lab tech that Eddy was friendly with at the police department. "I suppose that's like having his own badge and gun."

"It sure can be." Jo gave Samantha David's details then sprawled out on her couch. Samantha made a call to someone in police records. Her fingers flew across the keyboard as she waited for the information from her contact. A few minutes later, she hung up and spun around in her chair.

"Okay, he has a criminal history, but I'm sure you already knew that."

"I do."

"He was arrested for a minor job years ago,

but there's been no arrests or anything to indicate that he has been involved in the business for about twenty years."

"Maybe he just hasn't been caught."

"Maybe."

"He's a little hard to track. His social media is full of information about a gallery, but not much personal stuff."

"Anything interesting about the gallery."

"No, nothing that I can see." Samantha shook her head. "It doesn't look like I am going to find anything else for now, but I'll keep looking and let you know if I come across anything." Jo knew that with Samantha's background as an investigative journalist she would be the most likely to be able to dig up any dirt on David.

"Thanks, Sam."

"Anytime." Samantha smiled. "Will you meet us for lunch tomorrow? We're having a picnic."

"Sure, I think I can manage that. Thanks for

your help."

"No problem. Just stay on your toes, Jo."

"I will." Jo nodded. "I'll see you tomorrow." As she left Samantha's villa she felt more prepared for working out what was going on. David had his secrets, she was sure of it. Bruce mentioned that David was having financial trouble. She knew one person who could dig into his records and see if that was true. She walked straight towards Walt's villa. Since his car was in the driveway she assumed that he was home. She carefully wiped her feet on the mat outside his front door, then knocked twice. Walt opened the door and smiled.

"Jo, what a wonderful surprise."

"Hi Walt. I hope that you don't mind the drop-in."

"No, it's fine. You're always welcome." He held her eyes for a moment. "But this isn't a friendly visit is it?"

"Not exactly. I was hoping to get your help on

something."

"Sure, Jo." He gestured for her to step inside. Jo wiped her feet once more then followed him in. "What can I help you with?"

"I'm trying to help an acquaintance who's had something stolen and I need to see if you can get some financial information on someone for me."

"Ah, just give me the name."

She handed him a slip of paper and he walked over to his computer. "Is there a reason you want to know about David's finances?"

"He might be involved in some theft or insurance fraud, or both. I can't say much more than that."

"I understand. At least it's not some poor sap getting nabbed for buying candy and jewelry for another woman."

"Poor sap? If he's buying things for his mistress, I'd say the wife is the victim." She sat down in a recliner not far from his computer. "Don't you think?"

"I don't know. I used to think so, but as life gets longer, sometimes I wonder. What if you married the wrong one? What if you fall in love with someone else? Is that really such a terrible thing?"

"I wouldn't know." She shrugged and laughed.

"Nor would I." He winked at her. "But I can tell you that if I was married at my age I would want my freedom to choose what I did with my life. I wouldn't want to feel obligated to a decision that I made many years before."

"That is true. Life changes over the years, and it changes the person you are. But the courteous thing to do is end a relationship before starting another," Jo said.

"Maybe. I just don't know if it's that simple anymore." Walt continued to type. "People always think you can get married, and when it doesn't work out, you can just get divorced. But they never think about the finances. Marriage, sure, it's just a piece of paper, but what's beyond that is far more binding than any piece of paper could be. You own a house together, bank accounts together, debt together. It is endless and unraveling it all, especially late in life, is not an easy task."

"I've never really thought about that, but I guess you're right."

"Maybe that's why people stay together when they shouldn't."

"Maybe," Jo said.

"Well, from what I can tell he has a very bad credit rating. He's dodging bill collectors. His money must be very tight. He is up to his ears in debt." Walt continued to type information into the computer.

"That just confirms what my friend told me about him. Thanks Walt."

"Anytime. If I come across anything else, I'll let you know." He walked her to the front door. "Or if you want to share something else."

"That's it for now." She grinned.

"I'm always happy to help you."

"I know that, Walt. Thank you." She smiled.

"Yes, Jo thank you, I mean you're welcome."

Jo grinned as she closed the door behind her. On her way back to her villa she considered what information she had about David.

When she reached her villa she placed a few calls to some local fencing contacts. She wanted to be sure that Bruce wasn't still in the business. When she got hold of one particular contact her skin crawled with memories of her interactions with him.

"Well, well, nice to hear from you, Jo. Do you have something for me?"

"I'm not involved in that life anymore, Boggs."

"But you called. Is there something else you want from me?"

"Yes. Some information on a couple of people."

"Information? What, are you a cop now?"

"No, I just need some information."

"What for?"

"Are you going to help me?"

"Are you going to pay me?"

"If that's what it takes, then I will. But only if you actually have some information for me."

"Give me the names." She gave him David and Bruce's full names.

"All right, meet me at six. You know where to find me."

"Okay, I'll be there."

"Bring cash."

"Yes, Boggs." She rolled her eyes and hung up the phone. Although she wanted the information she wasn't sure if Boggs was telling her the truth and would give her the information if he had any, or if he was just baiting her so that he could see her in person. She glanced at her watch and saw that it was already late. She had missed lunch so she threw together an early dinner. As she ate she jotted down what she already knew about both Bruce and David. She also added her own thoughts about her experiences with Bruce. She wanted to believe that he was trustworthy, but her past made it impossible.

***

A few minutes before six Jo parked around the block from Boggs' office. He rented a small space, not a shop or a building, but just a tiny office without a sign. He hopped between three or four of the offices, but she always met him at the same one. As she suspected his beat-up motorcycle was parked in front of the office building. As she walked up to the door she prepared herself for what she might face. Boggs had a reputation for violent outbursts, especially if he wasn't shown the respect he believed he was owed. She pushed the door open and stepped inside to find Boggs crammed behind his desk. He was at least fifty pounds heavier than the last time she saw him.

"Jo, I wasn't sure if you'd show up."

"I wasn't sure if you actually had information for me." She sat down as far from his desk as she could manage.

"I do." He scrutinized her from across the desk. "But I'm not sure that I want to give it to you."

"I brought the money."

"Good. But that's not what I'm concerned about. I'm concerned about whether or not you're working with the cops."

"Boggs, please, you know me."

"Do I? It's been a long time since I've heard your voice or seen your pretty face. I thought we were friends?"

Jo gritted her teeth and lowered her eyes.

"Are you going to give me the information or not?"

"Watch your tone, girl."

"I'm hardly a girl." She laughed. "Aren't we

both a bit old for this, Boggs?" She sat forward and met his eyes. "I'm here to do business not play cat and mouse."

"Maybe you should play, if you want the information. Tell me about your life."

"No, I'm not here for small talk. I'm here for information, which I'm starting to see you don't have." She stood up from her chair.

"Sit down." He pointed to a chair closer to the desk. Jo froze where she stood and considered whether to turn and leave. If she did Boggs would be angry, but by the time he extricated himself from the desk she would be long gone. However, she would lose him as a contact, and that wasn't something that she wanted to risk. She sat down in the chair that he directed her to.

"Fine, I'm sitting."

"Good. You've lost some of your manners over the years."

"Or maybe I'm just not as easily intimidated."

"Maybe, but you should be. Perhaps you

forget how long my reach is?" He brushed a napkin across his upper lip to sop up the sweat that gathered there.

"I'm aware of your reach, Boggs, and I'm not here to disrespect you, but the information I need is time sensitive."

"All right. I didn't find much on Bruce, but David is definitely active."

"Who is he selling to?"

"I don't know. Things aren't like they used to be. Everything is digital now. Maybe he's selling on some website somewhere, I can't keep up with that technology. The point is, some of my customers have been sniffing around him lately, which means he's probably selling somewhere. Honestly, I'm upset about it, because he knows he should be going through me."

"But you don't think Bruce is involved?"

"If he is there's not even a whisper about it. How are you caught up in all of this? I thought you went straight."

"I did, I still am. Bruce asked for my help."

"Ah, I see. So, anything for Bruce, but not even a phone call for me?"

"I called you now didn't I?"

"I guess. Better late than never."

"If you come across any information about who David is selling to, give me a call, all right?" She wrote her number on a piece of paper and slid it across the desk to him.

"Are you going to answer?" He smiled at her as she backed away towards the door.

"For you, Boggs, of course."

As soon as Jo was outside the door of the office she thought about changing her number. Maybe if she wasn't so keen on finding out information about David, she would have. Boggs left a shiver down her spine that was hard to shake. She got into her car and drove back towards her villa. It was just dark. As she reached her villa the sounds of the frogs that populated the tall reeds around the water, filled the air. She took a breath of the scents that wafted from her garden before she stepped inside. Maybe there would be another way that didn't include relying on Boggs' information, but for now it was all that she had.

Chapter Three

When Jo woke the next morning she checked her phone right away. With no calls from anyone she was discouraged. So far she had no real leads, except information from Boggs which may or may not have been accurate. She logged into her computer and started doing some research on David. She wanted to find out as much information about him as possible. Engrossed in trying to find some new information she was startled when her cell phone rang.

"Hi Samantha."

"Did you forget?"

"Forget about what?"

"The picnic! I'm picking up burgers for everyone."

"Oh sorry, I guess I lost track of time. I'll be there."

"Great!"

After she hung up the phone she sent a text to Bruce.

Just an update- I am working on verification. I will text you when I have anything solid.

She tucked her phone into her purse then left her villa. The slope of the path that led down to the lake afforded her a view of the picnic table her friends used as a meeting place before she ever reached it. She could see Eddy already seated there, along with an assortment of brown paper bags. She smiled as she reached the table.

"Looks like lunch is already here."

"Yes, it is. Sustenance," Eddy said.

"I'm not sure it's nutritionally sound, but a good cheeseburger can really hit the spot sometimes," Jo said.

"If you like cheeseburgers you should go by

the community center tonight as they're having a special dinner, hot dogs and cheeseburgers for free," Eddy said.

"Mm, tempting. But I have to do a stakeout tonight."

"Oh?" Eddy handed her a cheeseburger then set the bag in the middle of the picnic table. "What kind?"

"It's something for a friend."

"The favor you mentioned?"

"Yes."

"Do you want company?"

She glanced up at him and smiled.

"Nice of you to offer, but no, I'll be fine."

"Is it in a safe part of town?"

She rolled her eyes.

"How did I know that was going to be your next question? Eddy, it's not the fifties anymore, I'm perfectly capable of taking care of myself."

"Careful now, I'd be just as worried about Walt if he was the one doing the stakeout."

"So would I!" She laughed and shook her head. "I'll be fine."

Samantha's laughter drew her attention to the path by the water. Walt and Samantha walked towards them with wide smiles on their faces.

"It took a little convincing, but I got him here."

"Well done!" Eddy smiled.

"Burgers!" Samantha grinned. "I've been looking forward to this." She plopped down on the bench beside Jo. "I made sure I got you a burger that you will like." She nudged Walt's side with her elbow.

"Thanks Samantha, but that doesn't change what the burger is made out of, does it?" He cringed.

"Just try not to think about it." Samantha patted his back.

"This looks delicious." Jo picked up her burger with both hands and took a big bite of it. A bit of the sauce trailed down her chin.

"Oh Jo, that's just...well how could you, here." Walt thrust a napkin towards her.

"Thanks, could you get it for me?" She tipped her chin towards him. His cheeks flushed as he patted at her chin with the napkin. She tried not to laugh.

"There, that's better." He sighed and picked up his burger. After a careful inspection to make sure that it was plain, well done, and lightly salted he took a bite.

As the four friends shared their junk food, Samantha updated them on the current happenings at Sage Gardens. "There's going to be an art auction to raise money for a cruise at the end of the year."

"A cruise?" Eddy scoffed. "That's just one more way to sucker money out of you."

"I think it would be fun." Samantha took a sip

of her soda.

"Cruises are notorious for spreading viruses." Walt shuddered. "Enjoy your cruise, because when you get home you're going to be erupting from both ends."

"Walt!" All three of his friends shouted at the same time.

"What?" Walt glanced around at them.

"We're eating." Jo scrunched up her nose.

"I could have mentioned that the chances of contracting severe illness from undercooked meat are just about equal to coming home from a cruise with a tummy ache."

"That's it, you're not allowed to talk until we finish our food." Eddy jabbed a finger at him. "Not another word."

Walt frowned and took another bite of his burger.

"Maybe Jo could tell us about her stakeout tonight instead?" Eddy met her eyes.

"A stakeout? You didn't tell me!" Samantha pouted. "I could have made muffins."

"No muffins, and no company." Jo shook her head. "This one I'm doing solo."

"Why? Wouldn't it be safer to have a second person with you?" Samantha picked up a french fry.

"I have my reasons. I'd appreciate it if you understood that."

"I do." Samantha finished her burger then wiped her hands together to brush off the crumbs. "But if you need anything, we're only a phone call away."

"I know." Jo smiled. "I'm glad you are."

"So, about this art auction? I assume that you're all going to participate?" Samantha asked.

"What is the point if I don't want to go on the cruise and I could care less about art?" Eddy shook his head.

"The point is I'm in charge of making sure

that we have enough people signed up to make the auction worthwhile." She pulled a small clipboard out of her purse. "So sign up!" Eddy eyed her for a moment then smiled.

"Anything for you, Samantha." He signed his name on the clipboard then handed it over to Walt along with the pen.

"Oh, I have my own." Walt reached in his pocket and pulled out a pen. "Do you have any idea how many germs are on pens?"

"I'd rather not know." Eddy chuckled. "Add it to the list of things you're not allowed to tell me."

"Okay." Walt signed his name and handed the clipboard to Jo. Jo took Eddy's pen and scribbled her name. Then she grabbed a napkin and scrubbed at her fingertips.

"Very funny." Eddy grinned.

"I've got to get going. But I'll be there for the art auction, Samantha."

"Actually, I hoped that you'd do a little more than that for me. I know you're busy, but if you have any spare time, do you think you could help me value some of the artwork? Just so we know which ones would be worth more than others. I know you have experience with art."

"Yes, I do." Jo noticed Eddy's cheeks flush. "Saturday afternoon, how does that sound?"

"Perfect. Thanks so much, Jo. I want this to be as professional as it can be."

"No problem." As Jo left the picnic table she knew that her friends were just a phone call away. But traveling back into her old life put them at a further distance. It would have been wise to have a second person on the stakeout with her, but she didn't want to risk anyone finding out who had asked her for help.

Chapter Four

Jo spent the rest of the afternoon preparing for the stakeout with plenty of good CDs, a stockpile of non-perishable snacks, and freshly polished miniature binoculars. Once she was equipped she headed off to take position.

The parking lot that was adjacent to the gallery's parking lot was large enough to tuck her car off to the side without drawing attention. Once she settled in she noticed that there was very little traffic. The gallery wasn't open that day, which made her think it would be the perfect night for the thief to strike. There would be little risk of getting caught. She bobbed her head to the music that filled the car and mulled over the possibility that David was involved in stealing the paintings. She wondered how Bruce would react when she gave him proof. The idea that he would turn David into the police was unlikely. He would handle it himself, and how he would handle it concerned her.

If she gave Bruce proof that David stole the paintings would David lose his life over it? Bruce never struck her as a violent man when they worked together, but time could change people. He had a lot to lose, and if he thought David was going to take it from him, he might just become someone she didn't expect him to be. As she considered this she noticed a group of people that walked towards the gallery. They laughed and shoved one another as they approached the building. Her interest heightened when she assessed that they were all quite young, perhaps in their teens. In her experience teens and their invincible mentality meant trouble was sure to follow.

As Jo suspected, one of the boys reached into his backpack and pulled out a few cans of spray paint. He tossed one to another boy, then pointed out the large glass window. None of them noticed her car tucked in the shadows of a large tree. If she scared them off she'd give away her position, and might possibly blow the stakeout. If she didn't, then Bruce might have quite a hefty bill if he had to replace the window. As the boy with the backpack neared the window, he must have touched the glass, because lights began to flash and an alarm blared so loud that Jo winced. The teens scattered in different directions. The alarm blared for a few more minutes, then shut off. She scrunched down in the car as she waited for a response to the alarm. Within five minutes a car rolled up to the front of the gallery. Bruce jumped out and slammed his car door shut then walked up to the front. She watched him for a moment, then fired off a text.

Don't worry, it was just a bunch of kids that set off the alarm. I'm watching.

Bruce pulled his phone out of his pocket, looked at it, then surveyed the parking lot. Jo flashed her lights just long enough to get his attention. Her phone buzzed with a text in return.

I see you. Let me know if anything happens tonight.

Jo fired a text back to let him know that she would. He got back into his car and drove off. She relaxed against the seat and took a deep breath. Now she knew that the alarm worked. That made her job a little easier as she didn't have to worry too much about someone sneaking in when she wasn't looking. However, if the alarm was that sensitive she had to wonder how David was sneaking in, and getting the paintings out of the gallery, without ever setting it off. Maybe he was disarming it. If he was using his code surely Bruce would immediately know it was him as there would be a record of it that would easily point to him as the thief. She made a mental note to ask Bruce about how the alarm was bypassed. Maybe David had another way of getting in and out without being detected. There was nothing to indicate a break-in which also made her suspect that David used his key. If he came in the front door in plain view, then she would have no problem spotting him.

As a few hours slid by Jo's mind churned over the recent events of her life. She'd settled into a new home in Sage Gardens, she'd made good friends who accepted her despite her past, and there was hope in her future for the first time in a very long time. She was glad she could help out Bruce as it was a fun addition to tending her garden and playing cards with Samantha late into the night.

As the daylight began to fade into darkness she was relieved to see that the lights in the parking lot clearly illuminated the entrance of the gallery. Since Bruce stopped by she hadn't seen another car in the parking lot, or any movement on the sidewalk in front of the gallery. Her mind drifted despite her usual ability to focus. Then something made her entire body jolt. She peered through the windshield at the large glass front of the gallery. Even though she hadn't seen anyone come or go, she was sure that she'd caught a glimpse of movement through the window. Maybe someone had slipped in when she wasn't looking? But why hadn't the alarm gone off? She stepped out of the car and crept towards the building. She'd just touched the side door when she heard a gunshot followed by the sound of shattering glass. Her heart dropped as she yanked at the door only to find that it was locked.

Jo ran around to the back door in time to see a figure in the distance. The person was too far for her to have any chance of catching up. She pulled open the back door and ran inside. A pool of blood spread across the center of the gallery floor. She covered her mouth to stifle a scream as she recognized who it belonged to. How had this happened while she sat outside watching the gallery? She leaned down and touched the side of Bruce's neck to check if there was a pulse. Her body trembled when she found none.

"Jo!" She jumped and spun around to see Eddy at the back door. "You've got to get out of here, the police are on their way."

"Eddy, what are you doing here?"

"Never mind that, just go. Now!"

"I can't, I can't leave him here like this." Sirens blared from outside and red and blue lights flashed through the windows. Jo couldn't move a muscle.

"You have to, Jo. If you're caught here it's going to look very bad." She took a deep breath and nodded. As she placed her hand on the doorknob, it was ripped away from her, and a police officer barged in with his gun drawn.

"Hands in the air! Both of you!" Eddy raised his hands in the air and took a slight step back. Jo's heart raced with panic. She glanced in every direction for a way out that didn't include handcuffs, but there was no other option. Reluctantly, she raised her hands in the air and stood beside Eddy. "Against the wall." The officer gestured to the nearby wall. Behind him another officer came in who spoke quickly into his radio. Jo glanced over at Eddy whose face was directed at the wall.

"What now?" Jo asked.

"Just keep your mouth closed, don't say a word. I'll do the talking."

She looked back at the wall and held her breath as the officer came closer to them.

"We're unarmed." Eddy laced his hands behind his head. "We found the body."

The officer began to pat down Eddy first, then he moved on to Jo. She cringed and held her breath, she felt so uncomfortable around the police. Paramedics rushed past them to check on Bruce. When the officer commanded it, Jo turned slowly around to face him. She didn't dare look him in the eye. Her mind flashed back to the years she spent in prison. She couldn't do that again, not even for a day.

"What happened here?" The officer took out

his notepad.

"Like I said, we found the guy on the floor." Eddy shrugged. "Not much more to say than that."

"Really?" The officer looked straight at Jo. "Is that your story, too?" Unable to form words even if she wanted to, Jo only nodded.

"We were just about to report it when you came in. Great response time you've got there," Eddy said.

The officer narrowed his eyes at Eddy. "And what exactly were you doing so close to the gallery when it was closed? What made you come inside?"

"We heard a gunshot." The words slipped past before Jo could think them through.

"Ah, well that's important information. What time did you hear the gunshot?"

"The same time someone called 911 to report one I'd assume." Eddy crossed his arms.

"Is there a reason why you're answering most of my questions?" The officer looked between Eddy and Jo. "Because it seems to me that you two are trying to hide things, which I can't understand, if you just happened upon this body. Do either of you know the victim?"

"Yes." Jo closed her eyes for a moment. "His name is Bruce, he owns the gallery."

Eddy nudged her foot with his, but she ignored him.

"You knew him?" The officer searched her eyes. She didn't know how to respond to his probe. If she lied it would incriminate her, if she told him the truth it would incriminate her. It wouldn't take long for them to figure out that not only was she helping out Bruce, but she had once worked with him on a heist. Once they put two and two together she would be behind bars. Maybe, if she could talk her way out of it for the moment she would have a chance to escape.

"Not exactly. He was going to show me a piece

of artwork after hours. But when my friend and I showed up to see it we heard a gunshot from outside. We rushed inside and found him like this," Jo said.

"Okay, I'll need you to give a complete statement, but for the moment I'm going to have you go outside with another officer. We need to make sure that the shooter isn't still in the building."

"I saw someone running away as I was coming inside, but they were already at the end of the street." Jo pointed in the direction the person ran.

"We still have to be sure."

Jo nodded. She turned and followed the officer without even looking at Eddy. Once they were outside the officer occupied himself with roping off the crime scene area.

"What happened to keeping quiet, Jo?" Eddy tried to meet her eyes, but she avoided them.

"You don't know what's going on here, Eddy. I'm in a lot of trouble."

"You'll be fine, Jo. You didn't kill him, you're innocent, the evidence will prove that."

"No, it won't." She wiped a hand across her face. "I wasn't completely honest. I do know Bruce well. In fact, we knew each other pretty well in my old life."

"Your old life? Oh." Eddy's voice dropped.

"Yes. It's only a matter of time before they figure out our connection. None of this will look good."

"Don't worry about it. I can talk to them. I'll explain that it was all just a coincidence."

"Eddy, that's sweet, and I know that you think you still have influence in police work, but the cops will want to make a collar, they are not going to care about what you have to say."

"What about security? Did your friend have cameras in the gallery?"

"Yes, he did." She breathed a sigh of relief. "Maybe that will clear me."

"I'm sure it will. But for now, don't volunteer any more information. No matter what he asks you, do your best to be polite but evasive."

"Don't you think that will make me look more suspicious?"

"You are going to be looking suspicious no matter what. Let them be suspicious. As long as they don't have anything to prove that you were involved it won't matter."

"Okay." She took a deep breath and nodded again. "I'll do my best."

"Good." He patted her shoulder. "Don't worry, Jo, you're not alone in any of this."

She swallowed hard. She wanted to believe him, but it was hard to, when she was so used to being alone. Another officer walked over to them.

"I need to check your hands."

"For gunpowder residue." Eddy frowned and held out his hands. Jo followed suit.

"Okay, you're both clear and neither of you

had a weapon on you. At this time you're free to go, but please remain in the area. We will be contacting you for more information."

"Yes, we will cooperate in any way that you need." Eddy offered his hand to the officer. "We only want to help."

"Good." The officer shook his hand, then offered his hand to Jo. Jo took it in a quick shake and turned away. Her body flared from the tips of her toes to the top of her head. Just having a police officer close to her was enough to set off a panic attack. Eddy curled his arm around her shoulders and steered her back towards her car.

"Just act casual. If you start to melt down, the police are going to be even more suspicious."

"I'm not going to melt down, Eddy. What are you even doing here? Did you follow me?" She glanced over at him. His jaw tensed and he nodded.

"Yes, I did. I know you're probably upset with me about that, but this is not the place to argue about it." He opened her car door for her. "Meet me at my villa and we can discuss it."

"No, I don't want to go to your villa, Eddy. I want to know why you followed me here." Jo sat down in her car.

"Fine, then Samantha's." Eddy nodded to her then closed the door. He adjusted his hat as he walked away from her. She noticed that he walked all the way to a parking lot at the end of the street before getting into his car.

Chapter Five

As Jo drove back to Sage Gardens she considered whether to just go back to her villa. She felt like she needed time to herself to comprehend what had happened. But she was too annoyed. She wanted to know why Eddy thought he needed to spy on her. She parked at her villa, then walked over to Samantha's. By the time she reached it Eddy pulled into the driveway right behind her. He got out of the car and jogged slowly after her.

"Jo wait, I want to explain."

"Go ahead." She crossed her arms as she turned to look at him. Eddy took a slight step back in reaction to the harshness of her stare.

"I was worried about you. I just wanted to make sure that you were safe."

"You knew, didn't you?"

He grimaced and glanced away from her. "I

didn't at first, but I overheard Walt and Samantha discussing the man you asked them to look into. When I did a background check on David I discovered what he was involved in. I followed you because I wanted to make sure that you weren't in over your head."

"I can handle myself, Eddy, you know that."

"Is that why Bruce is dead?" He searched her eyes. "Jo, if he came after you, and you did what you had to do, I understand that. You need to tell me the truth now, while we can still get ahead of this."

"If I what?" She stared hard into his eyes. "Are you asking me if I killed him?"

"I'm just letting you know that either way, I'm going to do whatever it takes to protect you."

"I didn't kill him, Eddy. I would never..." She lowered her eyes. "I didn't tell you the details because it wasn't supposed to be dangerous."

"But it was. What if whoever killed him decided to kill you, too?"

"You being there wouldn't have changed that. Eddy, I appreciate that you care about me, but you have to let me have my privacy."

"Fine." He nodded. "But if I wasn't there you would have still been standing over Bruce's body when the police walked in."

"Maybe." She brushed a hand back through her hair and stared down at the driveway. "I was in shock."

"You probably still are. Let's get inside." He knocked on the door. Samantha opened it with a surprised smile.

"Eddy, Jo, what's going on?"

"We need to talk." Eddy tipped his head towards the door. "Can we come in?"

"Of course." She stepped back. As Jo walked past her she gasped. "Jo, you look terrible. Are you okay? What happened?" She ushered them both into the living room.

"I was on the stakeout and someone managed to get past me into the gallery. Whoever it was killed Bruce, and the police arrived shortly after I got inside."

"Oh Jo, I'm so sorry. You were friends with Bruce."

"Knowing that I might go to jail for his murder makes it a little worse. Do you mind if I clean up in your bathroom?" Jo asked.

"Of course not, go right ahead." Samantha sat down on the couch beside Eddy.

"I'll fill her in while you're gone," Eddy said.

Jo nodded, but didn't say a word. She was still a little annoyed that Eddy followed her. Every time she thought he trusted her, he proved that he didn't. She looked in the mirror and washed her hands. She splashed water on her face. Her mind flicked with thoughts of Bruce. How could she have missed him and his killer going into the gallery? Maybe he thought he was safe, because she was outside. She closed her eyes for a moment as she processed the memory of finding him in the gallery. Was there something she had overlooked?

When she returned to the living room Samantha and Eddy were sitting on the couch. Samantha looked up at Jo.

"How frightening that you were so close when this happened. I'm so glad that you're okay."

"That remains to be seen." Jo wiped her hands dry on her jeans and sat down in a chair across from them. "I'm pretty sure I'm the police's number one suspect."

"That may be true, but it won't be that way for long. The cameras will clear you." Eddy stood up. "If they thought you did it, you wouldn't be sitting here in Samantha's living room, you'd be sitting in an interrogation room."

"They have to have something to make an arrest right?" Jo shrugged. "Give them time."

"Jo, you can't think so negatively about this. Try to focus on the positive," Samantha said.

"You sit in a prison cell for years, and tell me to focus on the positive." Jo winced as soon as the words left her mouth. "I'm so sorry, Samantha. I didn't mean that. I'm just a little on edge."

"No you're right. You have a right to be scared. I know what's on the line for you. But we're here to make sure that nothing bad happens. For the record, I had no idea that Eddy was following you."

"It was Walt's idea." Eddy frowned. "He told me I should just keep an eye on you in case you needed a little back-up."

"Walt?" Jo shook her head and smiled. "I should have known. He's always doing something from behind that curtain of his."

"Curtain?" Samantha raised an eyebrow.

"Walt presents this docile image, but behind it he's quite clever and stubborn."

"I can agree on both counts." Eddy chuckled.

"Look Eddy, I'm not upset with you for being there, I just think it's important that you trust me enough to be able to handle myself."

"I do trust you, Jo. I also value you, which is

why I wanted to make sure that you were safe. Heck, if I was on a stakeout I'd bring you with me to keep me safe."

"Or me." Samantha smiled.

"Yes, or you." Eddy smiled in return. "My point is, it's not about you being a woman if that's what you think, Jo. It's that you're a lone wolf that never asks for help, even when you think you might need it."

"You have me there." She nodded. "I guess we're going to find out more about all of this in the morning."

"You can sleep here tonight, Jo."

"Thanks Samantha, but I'd rather go home. I just need to sort some things out in my mind. I want to make sure I'm ready for the interview with the detective tomorrow."

"That's a good idea. But don't worry, they'll have the surveillance tapes by then and all of this will be a bad memory."

"I hope so." Jo bit into her bottom lip. As they

spoke Eddy's cell phone rang. He glanced at the screen.

"It's Chris. I asked him to look into things for me at the station and let me know when there was any news on the case." He put the phone to his ear. "Chris, what do you have for me?"

"It's not good, I'm afraid."

"What do you mean?"

"I mean, the tapes you were waiting for don't exist."

"How is that possible? Jo said there were cameras all around the gallery, inside and out."

"And there were, but they were all disabled during the time of the murder. There's nothing on the tapes. The fact that Jo knew they were there only means that she might have disabled them."

"Oh, this just keeps getting worse, doesn't it?"

"Just try to keep your friend calm. I can tell you that there are some other reasons to suspect her, so be prepared for that."

"What other reasons?"

"I don't know exactly. I just know that she's suspect number one at the moment."

"Thanks Chris." Eddy shook his head as he hung up the phone. He took a deep breath then turned to look at Jo. "Is there something else I should know about your involvement with Bruce?"

"Why? What did Chris say?" Jo's eyes narrowed.

"Just answer my question first, please." Eddy set his jaw.

Jo turned away from him and stared hard out the window. She didn't want to admit to anything, but she knew that she needed to tell him the truth.

"We worked together years ago."

"Okay," Eddy said slowly.

"What about the cameras? Did they see who did it?"

"The cameras were disabled."

"Of course they were." Jo's shoulders drooped. "The thief has been disabling the cameras when he steals the paintings."

"What thief and what paintings?" Eddy placed a hand on her shoulder. "I'm only trying to help, Jo."

"There's nothing you can do." She sighed. "It's over now."

"What's over?" Eddy looked between Samantha and Jo. "What are you talking about, Jo?"

"Look, there's a bit of history between Bruce and me. I offered to help him figure out who has been stealing paintings from his gallery. He suspected his partner. All I needed to do was catch whoever broke into the gallery at night. Clearly, that did not go well. Now Bruce is dead and I'm going to be the one that they charge with his murder. I have no way to defend myself."

"Sure you do. Bruce asked you for help," Samantha said. "Don't worry, Jo, it looks bad, but we'll get it all worked out. The important thing is that you are safe, and we're going to keep you that way. Right Eddy?"

"Right." Eddy rested his hands on her shoulders and patted them twice. "You're in good hands, Jo, try not to stress about it. Go home, get some sleep, and we'll go from there."

"Okay. Yes, it would be good to get some sleep."

As Jo walked back to her villa every move she made was strange, as if it was performed by someone else. She was numb from the inside out. If the cameras couldn't clear her, and the police figured out her connection to Bruce, she would be locked up in no time. She went through the routine of brushing her teeth as if she was going to bed, but she didn't change out of her clothes. Instead, she stretched out on her bed fully dressed. She stared at the ceiling and willed it to give her another solution. She'd built a life at Sage Gardens, a life that she'd come to value beyond anything she had in the past. Even though

Samantha, Eddy, and Walt, were not family they were the closest to it that she'd ever experienced. Now she was faced with giving all of that up. However, there was no other answer.

With each hour that slipped past on the digital clock beside her bed, Jo got closer to being arrested. Given her connection to the victim she would arrest herself if she was a cop. Could she really just lay there and wait for the police car to show up? Her mind flooded with memories of being behind bars. She promised herself on the day that she became a free woman that she would never end up there again. All she had to do was tell Bruce no. If she'd done that she wouldn't be in this position. Instead she'd taken the risk, and the consequence was harsh. There was only one way out. She sat up in bed and looked around her sparse bedroom. There wasn't much to pack as she never let herself get too attached to things. However, she would miss her garden.

Jo scribbled a note to her friends and asked Samantha to look after her garden even though she knew that her garden probably had more chance of staying alive without Samantha's intervention. Then she threw some clothes and other items into a bag and headed out into the early morning air. It was still dark enough that not a single soul would witness her walking away. Within fifteen minutes she was at the bus station. She purchased a ticket for the next bus that would leave the station, then she sat down to wait. As the minutes dragged by she tried not to think about what she was leaving behind.

Chapter Six

Eddy glanced at his watch, then looked over at Samantha. "Knock again."

"Maybe she's sleeping, Eddy, we shouldn't wake her."

"I want to talk to her before she has to go down to the station. Knock again." Samantha sighed but she knocked again. "She's not opening. She's probably not here."

"I've already called her cell phone three times and she didn't answer. If she's not home then where is she? The police told her not to leave the area. It's barely daylight, where could she have gone?"

"Eddy, you know Jo isn't going to let anyone keep tabs on her. She has to be beside herself with worry. Maybe she is inside and she doesn't want to be bothered right now."

"I'm going in." Eddy aimed his shoulder

towards the door.

"Wait, don't!" Samantha pushed her hands against his arm before he could lunge forward. "I have a key. I don't think it's right for us to use it, but if you're that worried then I trust your instincts."

"Okay, open it up." He tilted his head towards the door. Samantha fished her keys out of her purse and found Jo's key. She slid it into the lock and opened the door. It made her a little sick to let herself into the home of someone who was so private, but she reminded herself that she did it to calm Eddy's nerves and make sure that Jo was safe.

"I'll take a look around. She could be sleeping." She put up a hand to keep Eddy from following her. "She is entitled to her privacy."

Eddy frowned but nodded. As he lingered by the door Samantha walked through the living room to the closed bedroom door. She knocked lightly. "Jo? Are you in there? It's Samantha."

After a few seconds with no response she opened the door. The moment she did she knew that something was very wrong. Jo's clothes were strewn on the floor, her closet door hung open with jackets and shoes tossed everywhere. Her heart dropped as she looked towards the bed. To her relief it was empty. On the bedside table was a note. She picked it up and read it over. Her throat grew dry as she recognized the implication of what she'd found.

"She's gone, isn't she?" Eddy stood in the bedroom door.

"Eddy, I told you to wait outside."

"I did. If I waited any longer, would you have hidden that note from me?" He plucked it from her grasp. "I know she's your friend, Samantha, she's my friend, too, but she's also now a prime suspect in a murder. If she takes off, she's proving her guilt."

"I don't blame her for running, Eddy. She's scared."

"I know, I don't blame her either. But I have to go get her."

"We don't even know where she is."

"She wouldn't fly, and she wouldn't drive far, she'd get on a bus. It gives her the chance to be anonymous and gets her where she's going with minimal security." He glanced at his watch. "She probably hasn't boarded yet. I'm going to get her right now."

"Wait Eddy, I'm going with you."

"I don't think that's a good idea, Samantha." He crumpled the note up in his hand. "We're going to have to move fast if we're going to catch her."

"Let's go then." Samantha hurried him out the door to his car. She paused only to lock Jo's door. That's when it struck her. If they hadn't gone inside, she might never have seen Jo again. If they didn't get to the bus station in time, she would be gone forever. She ran to the car and jumped in the passenger side just before Eddy threw the car into reverse. He floored it out of Sage Gardens, drawing looks of annoyance from those that walked their pets early, and the joggers that never seemed to sleep.

"Eddy, the speed limit is..."

"We're not doing the speed limit today, Samantha." As soon as he was on the main road he sped up even more. Samantha clutched the handle above the passenger window and did her best not to think about the dangers of his driving. She'd driven a little wild many times in pursuit of a story, but it was rare for her to be the passenger. It was hard to keep from crying out when he narrowly missed a large delivery truck that he cut off. They reached the bus station far faster than she thought was possible. When he parked he looked towards the bus station. "You're going to stay here."

"What? Why? I want to talk to Jo," Samantha said.

"No. I need to talk to her alone."

"Eddy, she's not going to be pushed around."

"I have no intention of pushing her around, but she needs someone to give her the hard truth, Samantha. She needs to know what's going to happen to her if she takes off and becomes a fugitive."

"All right, I'll stay here, but remember she's our friend, Eddy, not a criminal."

"I know that, Sam." He looked over at her with a soft frown. "I do."

Samantha watched him walk towards the bus station with long determined strides. He looked exactly like the police officer that he'd once been. In these matters she did her best to trust him, but she worried that Jo would not react well to his hard-nosed nature.

Eddy pulled open the door to the bus station and looked through the few faces that waited for the early bus. It wasn't long before he pinpointed Jo in the corner with her back to the wall. He ducked behind a partition before she could spot him in return. After a deep breath he walked towards her. Within a few steps she noticed him.

"Go home, Eddy."

"No." He sat down beside her. "I'm not going anywhere, and neither are you."

"Eddy, you can't stop me." She set her jaw and stared at the other people that waited in the bus terminal. "I have to do what's best for me, and that's to get as far away as fast as I can."

"You can't do that, Jo. It will only make you look guilty."

"I don't need to make myself look guilty. I already look guilty. The cameras were off, Eddy. There's no way to prove that it wasn't me that killed Bruce. Even you asked me if I did it."

"I asked you that because I'm an old cop, and it's just in my blood to ask the hard questions. I shouldn't have asked, but I did. It doesn't mean that you can't trust me."

"Well, then what does it mean? That you think I could possibly be a murderer?" She locked eyes with him.

"No, that's not what I thought. I thought maybe Bruce attacked you and you defended yourself. But I knew that you would never have hurt him without reason. I know you better than that."

"You say that, but you know about my past. I'm sure it crossed your mind that I might have killed him."

"No." He looked straight back into her eyes. "Not for a second. What I do know is that you're afraid of going back to prison and that you're about to make the stupidest decision that you could make. The moment you get on that bus, you'll have no chance of defending yourself."

"Like I will if I stay?" She blinked back tears and shook her head. "They're going to lock me up without a second thought."

"That's not how it works."

"It will be for me. It's a second offense, and a worse crime than the one I was imprisoned for.

No judge is going to care that I've turned my life around."

"So we don't rely on the judge. The easiest way to prove that you're not guilty is to find the person who is. But we're going to need your help in order to do that. You're the one that knew Bruce, and who his contacts might be."

"Eddy, I think my best bet is getting on that bus. Are you really going to stop me?"

"Yes, I am." He put his hand over hers. "I can't not stop you, Jo. You're going to ruin your life if you flee. You will lose all credibility in the eyes of the judge."

"How can I have any credibility once he looks into my past?"

"He's also going to look at the life that you live now, Jo. He's also going to see how you've stayed out of trouble all of this time. That counts, too. But not if you take off now when you need to stay and defend yourself."

"I don't know if you're right about that, Eddy.

It feels more like I'm a sitting duck."

"Maybe it feels that way to you, but I'm going to make sure that's not what happens. I know that I'm asking you to take a risk, I'm asking you to trust me."

"I do trust you, Eddy." She sighed and looked towards the bus that pulled up outside the terminal. "I guess the easy answer isn't always the right answer. That's one thing I've learned throughout my life."

"I can agree with that. Your life, the one that you've built here is worth fighting for."

"Yes, it is." She stood up from the bench. "I don't want to give it up without a fight."

"Let me take you home. Samantha's in the car, she can take your car home."

"Are you afraid I'm going to bolt again?"

"Shouldn't I be?" He offered a half-smile.

"I'm starting to think that you know me too well, Eddy."

"Maybe I do." He held out his arm to her. She took it and let him lead her out of the bus station. Samantha rushed up to both of them the moment they stepped outside.

"Are you okay, Jo?"

"She will be, once I get her home. Can you drive her car back?" He held out Jo's keys to her.

"Sure. Jo, I'll see you soon." Jo nodded at Samantha then climbed into the passenger seat of Eddy's car. As soon as the doors were closed Eddy started the engine.

"So now that we have agreed that you're going to fight, let's talk about a plan of action."

"I really don't want to talk about anything right now, Eddy. Can we just drive?" Eddy shifted the car into gear and nodded. During the drive home Eddy peppered a few questions into the silence between them, but Jo only stared out through the window. Her mind raced with all of the reasons she should have gotten on the bus. It was a good thing that Eddy drove her back to her villa, as if she was in her own car she might have headed for Canada instead.

Chapter Seven

When Eddy parked in Jo's driveway she was relieved to see her home, but also anxious.

"Thanks for the ride, Eddy." She started towards her door.

"Wait a minute." Eddy got out of the car and followed after her. "I want to talk to you about this."

"Not now, Eddy, I'm tired."

"The police already have a head start on us. It's almost eight, they're going to be investigating, we need to be, too."

"Eddy, you've helped enough."

Samantha pulled up with Jo's car and climbed out in time to see Eddy catch Jo's elbow.

"I haven't even begun to help. We need to talk this through."

"I said I appreciated your help, Eddy. I can take it from here."

"No, you can't."

"Jo? What's going on?" Samantha walked up to both of them.

"Samantha, I need some time to properly talk with Jo alone," Eddy said.

"What? Why?" Samantha started to move towards Jo's side.

"I have my reasons." He met Samantha's eyes. "Just let me do what I need to do."

"If that's what it will take to get both of you out of my driveway then fine." Jo sighed and unlocked her door. She stepped inside and Eddy followed right after her. He closed the door behind him. Samantha stood outside, uncertain of what to do. She trusted Eddy, but she also knew that Jo was the type that didn't like to be cornered.

"What do you want from me, Eddy?" Jo turned to face him. "There's nothing to investigate, you and I both know that."

"No, I don't know that. I'm sure there's plenty

to investigate. But we're not going to get anywhere with the investigation if you don't talk to me first."

"I don't know anything. If I knew who killed Bruce I'd tell you."

"You know more than you think. You're the only link here. If we talk it through, you might remember something that can help."

Jo sat down on the couch and stared at the carpet beneath her feet. "I guess I just don't know what to say. I feel so responsible for all of this."

"I know that you're upset, but you have to push that out of your mind. We need facts and information right now."

"Like what?"

"Okay, tell me about Bruce. What was he like?"

"I didn't know him that well personally. Our connection was only professional."

"Professional. What jobs did you do together?"

"It was only one job. We worked together on a heist. He covered for me and got me out of a very hairy situation. That's why I was willing to help him out."

"It didn't bother you that he was from your past?"

"Of course it did, but he turned his life around, just like I did. Who was I to judge him? He asked me to help him because he trusted me. As an ex-con, I know how rare it is to find someone that you can trust to help you. So when we bumped into each other and he told me what was happening I agreed to help."

"I hope you know that you can trust me, Jo." Eddy held her gaze.

"I know. I know I can trust you, and Samantha, and Walt, but none of you understand what it's like to be in prison and just how important it is for me to stay out of it. That's something I hope that none of you ever understand, but it does create some distance between us."

"I might not know what it's like, but I do know how serious it is and how easily a case can go awry. I have your back, Jo, but we have to work together to solve this case."

"I'm here. Any information you want, just ask."

"What about David? Did you know him?"

"I met him once a long time ago. I looked into him, as Bruce suspected he was the one stealing the paintings. Bruce's guess was that David stole the paintings to sell on the black market, and then claim it on the gallery's insurance."

"Double dipping." Eddy nodded. "That makes sense."

"Yes, it does. It's plenty of motive for him to kill Bruce also. If he thought Bruce was on to him then maybe he decided to kill him so that his crime would never be revealed."

"I don't know." Eddy frowned. "That's a big step to take. From a thief to a murderer?"

"It's happened before."

"Maybe, but we can't be sure that it was David. I think we need to know more about him. Did Bruce mention anyone else that was giving him any trouble?"

"No, he was only focused on David."

"Do you know of anyone from your shared past that might have had a grudge against Bruce?"

Jo closed her eyes and shook her head. "I try not to even think about it."

"Now you need to. Did Bruce have any enemies that you know of?"

"There were some people who were rivals, but these were thieves, not murderers."

"Maybe he crossed someone in the past, after you were out of his life."

"That's possible." She shook her head. "It feels like another lifetime now."

"I can have Samantha look into Bruce's and David's background. I can also get Chris to check up on David, see if he can get any information on him. If there's something to find, we'll find it."

"Great. I have some contacts I can reach out to."

"I'd be careful with that. We don't want the police getting wind of you reaching out to people from your past. It may look suspicious to them. Your job right now is to stay calm, keep your head down, and rely on your friends."

Jo took a deep breath and nodded. "I'll try."

"Good. And Walt will keep an eye on you."

"What?" She laughed.

"I'm serious." Eddy picked up his phone. "He's going to be your bodyguard until all of this is over. Whoever killed Bruce might know that he talked to you, or might have recognized you from a past connection. Walt will make sure you follow my advice not to contact people from your past."

"I don't need a babysitter, Eddy." She stood up and crossed her arms.

"Maybe not." He stood up as well. "But you're going to have one." He smiled. "Walt will be here in a few minutes. I suggest you sit back and let him clean your house."

Jo glanced around the mess she'd made when she packed the items she needed to take with her on the bus. "I suppose that could be a plus."

"I'll update you as soon as I know anything, Jo."

As Eddy stepped out of the villa, Samantha stepped back inside. She shot him an annoyed look then hurried over to Jo.

"Did he intimidate you?"

"No." Jo laughed. "Eddy only thinks he's scary." Samantha hugged her.

"I'm so glad he got to you before you got on that bus. What would I do without you?"

"I'm sure that you would be just fine."

"Your garden certainly wouldn't. You know I can't keep things alive."

"Okay, that's a good point." Jo smiled. "I'm sorry for trying to take off on you, I just thought it was the best thing to do."

"I understand why you did. I can't imagine how frightened you are. But you're not alone anymore, we're here to help you."

"I see that now." Jo glanced past her to the front door as Walt opened it. "It's wonderful to have such good friends."

"I'll go get us some breakfast." Samantha smiled as she headed out the door past Walt. Walt locked eyes with Jo as he stepped further into the house.

"Is it true?"

"Which part?" Jo picked up some of the napkins that were knocked off the kitchen counter when she rushed out the door. When she straightened up Walt was right beside her.

"That you were going to leave?" He looked into her eyes again.

"I thought I had to, Walt. I still think it might

have been a better idea."

"You weren't even going to say goodbye?" He leaned against the counter and lowered his eyes. "When Eddy told me, I didn't believe it. But I guess he was right."

"I left a note." Jo frowned. "I know that probably seems cold."

"I just thought, it's silly." He sighed and plucked the napkins out of her hands. "Can't use these now, they've been on the floor." He tossed them into her trash can.

"Walt, don't be upset with me."

"I'm not, I just, I don't know, I thought we were worth more to you than that."

"You are. I stayed, didn't I?" She smiled. He turned to look at her, his expression still solemn.

"What if Eddy hadn't shown up? Would you have stayed?"

"I don't know." She brushed her fingertips along the counter. "I wanted to, Walt, more than anything I wanted to stay. I love it here, and my friendship with all of you. But, if you want me to be honest with you, I'd do anything to stay out of prison."

"I wouldn't let you go to prison."

"That's what Eddy said." She laughed. "You two seem to think you can control the police and the court system."

"That's not what I think. I just know that I would do anything to keep you out of prison, too, Jo. All you had to do was trust us."

"I'm here." She met his eyes. "I didn't take off."

His lips finally cracked into a smile. "Yes, you are. So let's start figuring out who the real killer is. Can I use your computer?"

"Sure." She turned it on for him, then stepped back out of his way. Walt began tapping on the keys and didn't stop until Samantha returned with bagels.

"Breakfast!" She smiled. Jo couldn't help but

wonder if Samantha thought this was fun. She loved a good mystery and with her investigative instincts from when she was a reporter she probably saw the case as a challenge. If only she could see it that way, too. "A contact e-mailed me the financial records for David. I asked him to see if he could try to get them when Jo asked me about David and they were just sent through." Walt moved out of the way and Samantha opened the attachments.

"I don't know how you manage to get the things you do, but this should be helpful." Walt smiled as he looked at them.

"Don't you want to eat first, Walt?" Samantha asked.

"In a minute," Walt said distractedly as he scanned through the documents. Jo nibbled at her bagel as she watched Walt. By the time she finished her bagel Walt walked over to the table and began to fill them in on what he had found.

"It looks like David might be in debt, but that

hasn't stopped him from spending. Buying lavish gifts for females," Walt said.

"Really, as far as I know David's single, never been married."

"Hmm. Well, he has a girlfriend. There are several transactions at a female clothing store, lots of eating out in an amount that would most likely cover two meals."

"But I thought he was broke. He was in debt," Samantha said.

"This might be why he's broke. Whoever he is dating has rather expensive taste." Walt nodded.

"Interesting." Jo frowned. "So he's bleeding himself dry to please his girlfriend. It doesn't make sense to me that he would go to such lengths, even putting his business at risk, over a woman."

"You're not a man." Walt winked at her. "It depends on the woman."

"Oh, is that so?" Jo grinned.

"Yes, it is. A good woman can make a man do many things he never imagined he would."

"I agree." Samantha walked towards the computer and looked past him at the computer screen. "Is there any way to tell who he was dating?"

"Sorry, not from this information." He shook his head as he turned back to the computer. "But I can tell you they had dinner at LaRuse last week to the tune of four hundred dollars."

"Four hundred dollars? For two meals?" Jo's eyes widened.

"They probably just got appetizers," Samantha said.

"Ugh, you've got to be kidding me." Jo flopped back in the chair. "Anyone who pays that much for a meal has to have lost their mind."

"Especially if that person is in the financial bind that David is in. Maybe he's a fool, but I'd say he definitely has motivation here to make some extra money."

David had a very high-maintenance girlfriend despite his financial crisis. Even though the finances pointed to him as the thief, his motive struck Jo as weak. Would he really steal from his own business just to provide for a woman whose demands outpaced his means? Would David kill Bruce because Bruce found out that he was stealing?

"So, it's clear that David is in a bad financial place. However, I checked the finances for the gallery and it is not in as bad shape as Bruce claimed."

"He said it was a struggle to keep the doors open," Jo said as she set a bagel down on Walt's plate and peered past him at the computer.

"It's not raking in funds, but it has a good base to keep going for several years."

"I wonder why Bruce would say that then?"

"Have you considered the possibility that Bruce was the one stealing the paintings?" Walt wiped a bit of butter from the corner of his mouth.

"No, I honestly hadn't." Her eyes widened at the thought. "Why would he pin it on David?"

"To throw everyone off track maybe. To frame David for the thefts so that he could get David out of the business and keep the profits for himself?" Samantha suggested. "It's not unheard of, because partnerships usually include clauses that if one of the partners does anything to harm the business their interest in the business can be dissolved. Isn't that right, Walt?"

"Yes. Maybe Bruce wanted David out and thought he could use you to prove that David was stealing the paintings."

"That still swings David right back into the position of the main suspect in Bruce's death. If David figured out what he was doing, then he would have plenty of motive to kill Bruce."

"You're right. What exactly did you see last night, Jo?" Walt met her eyes. "Anything unusual?"

"A few hours before the murder a group of

teenagers set off the alarm and Bruce showed up to check on it. I let him know what happened and he went home."

"Or you thought he did," Samantha said.

"I saw his car pull away."

"Maybe he went around behind the building and slipped inside while the alarm was being reset? Maybe he planned to steal paintings right under your nose?" Walt said.

"Maybe." She sighed. "I'd hate to think that my judgment is so off."

"It happens to the best of us, Jo," Samantha said.

Jo nodded, but she didn't agree. It never happened to her. If Bruce played her, then he might have inadvertently or even intentionally framed her for his own murder. If she couldn't prove that David was the killer then she was going to get familiar with bars blocking her view of everything once more.

Chapter Eight

Eddy paced back and forth in his living room and pressed the phone to his ear. He'd been waiting for Chris to pick up the phone for several minutes. Each minute that slipped by felt like an eternity with the pressure of knowing that at any minute Jo would be picked up for questioning.

"Eddy, sorry you had to wait, it's really hopping in here today."

"It's not a problem, Chris. Can you run me a list of anyone currently in prison or previously charged with a crime that was a known associate of Bruce's?"

"I can, but it's going to take me some time. Do you think this had something to do with some bad blood?"

"I think it might. I'm worried that the detective on the case might be a little too focused on just Jo. I'd like to scrounge up some more options for him."

"Will do. I'll let you know as soon as I have anything. There's something I shouldn't tell you, Eddy."

"What's that?"

"Officers are going to pick Jo up for questioning in about an hour."

"Thanks Chris. Thanks for the help."

"If you say she's innocent I believe you, Eddy, I'll do what I can to help."

Eddy hung up the phone then dialed Samantha's number. He filled her in on the request he made of Chris. "That should give us a good base to start from. But since you can't start looking into any of those people until we have the list, maybe you can find something else?"

"I will do what I can."

"Sam, I'm coming over there to get Jo."

"For what?"

"She has to go in for an interview, and I'm going with her. I don't want her to get picked up by a patrol car, I'm going to take her in myself."

"Eddy, do you think she'll go?"

"I'm not sure. But I hope so."

After he hung up the phone he drove over to Samantha's villa. When he opened the door Jo turned to look at him with her face paler than he'd ever seen it.

"I don't have a choice, Jo, you are either going to be picked up by a patrol car, or you can let me drive you in, but you have to go in to speak to the police."

She took a deep breath and nodded. "I knew this was coming."

"If you'd rather wait, we can."

"I'd rather go in with you, Eddy. I know you have my back."

"Good. Then let's go. Don't forget that they can't have any proof against you, because you're innocent. Don't let them con you into admitting anything, or saying anything more than you need to."

"I think I can handle it. I have no choice but to face this."

Eddy walked with her to the car and opened the door for her. Jo hesitated for a moment before getting in, then she settled in the seat. When he closed the door she gritted her teeth. Eddy was right, running wasn't an option. The drive to the police station was short, and quiet. She stared out the window at all of the places in town she was used to visiting. Would she have a chance to visit any of them again? Her stomach tightened. Eddy parked, and then looked over at her.

"Are you okay?"

"I will be when this is over."

"You're going to be fine."

"Or I'm going to be behind bars."

"No Jo, you're coming home with me."

"If you say so, Eddy."

"I do." He rested his hand on her shoulder as

he led her into the front of the police station. As soon as they were inside Jo walked up to the desk, gave her name and said that she wanted to speak to the detective in charge of Bruce's case. Within moments she was escorted back to one of the interrogation rooms. She was whisked inside before Eddy had the chance to plead his case to go in with her. In some ways that was a relief to her. An officer remained in the room with her as they waited for the detective. A few minutes later the door opened and a man in his thirties stepped into the room. He wore a brown suit and a gaudy gold watch that clanged on the table as he sat down across from her.

"I'm Detective Rowan. I appreciate you coming in so willingly to talk with me."

"Of course, yes." She nodded.

"Are you nervous?" He smiled as he looked into her eyes. Jo wasn't sure how to take his friendly nature.

"A little."

"No need to be. I just need to straighten a few things out."

"Okay." Jo's muscles relaxed a little. Detective Rowan appeared to have very little interest in her as a suspect. "Anything I can do to help."

"I've done a little bit of research on you, Jo. Of course we have to do that with anyone that's involved in a crime."

"I wasn't involved."

"Even if you're just a witness."

"I honestly didn't witness much."

"I'm sure you can understand, this is all so we can catch a killer. Now, I noticed that you and Bruce have quite a bit of history together."

"Some."

"More than some, right?" He smiled as he looked up from the file in front of him. "It was suspected that you two were up to no good together before you were arrested."

"That was a long time ago."

"And yet, you were in his gallery when he was killed."

"After he was killed."

"You just happened to be there to look at a piece of art?"

"My friend and I were going to see a particular portrait."

"So, Bruce didn't ask you to look into some stolen paintings for him?"

Jo froze. She didn't expect the detective to know that and wasn't certain how to respond to the question. "Uh, I was helping a friend."

"How nice for you, but that wasn't the question that I asked, was it?" His tone and demeanor shifted from friendly to stern. "Were you investigating something for Bruce?"

"No, not really." She cleared her throat. "I was just helping him out."

"So you lied about the reason that you were at the gallery."

"I thought it would be easier not to mention it."

"Easier? It's easier to lie than to tell the truth?"

"I offered to help an old friend out by looking into something for him, but I didn't have any way to prove it so I wasn't sure if it was something I should mention."

"Now, don't try to pretty it up, Jo. You lied to a police officer. So, how can I know that you didn't lie about everything else?"

Jo narrowed her eyes as she realized she'd fallen right into his trap.

"I didn't kill him, I have nothing else to say."

"Nothing? What about an explanation as to why you got yourself involved with a known felon?"

"He asked me for help, I wanted to help him."

"Why? Because you were still in contact? From the paperwork we found at the gallery it looks like paintings have been going missing. Did you partner up with Bruce so that you could steal his paintings? Maybe he wasn't giving you enough of the cut and you decided to take him out?"

"I am out of that life, and even if I wasn't, I would never kill anyone."

"Sure, because a thief has too many morals to do something like that."

Jo stood up from the table and locked eyes with the detective. "Are you going to arrest me?"

"If I could, believe me I would. Just give me a little time, we'll get there."

"You're wrong." She shook her head. "You're wasting your time on me while the murderer gets away with the crime."

***

Eddy stared at the closed door. He thought about suggesting that Jo get a lawyer, but he wanted to find out how the questioning had gone first. He knew that Jo had enough experience to protect herself and getting a lawyer often antagonized the police. As he waited for the interview to be over he leaned against the wall outside the interrogation room. As officers milled about and phones rang he felt at home for the first time in a long time. Before he retired he had spent most of his life in a police station. The smells, sounds, and surroundings of it were more familiar to him than any place he'd ever lived. The sharp sound of his cell phone jolted him out of his memories. He answered it the moment that he saw that it was Chris.

"Hey Chris."

"I only have a minute to talk."

"I'm here at the police station..."

"No, we can't be seen together. You've got to be careful. I e-mailed the list of names to you. At this time the detective on the case only has circumstantial evidence, but he likes Jo for this, and I don't doubt he'll be coming after you next."

"I'm not worried about him, he has nothing on me. But Jo..."

The door to the interrogation room swung open and Jo pushed past Eddy towards the lobby.

"Chris, I have to go." Eddy hung up the phone and followed after Jo. She didn't stop until she was outside the front doors. Only then did she allow Eddy to catch up with her.

"Jo, are you okay?"

"No, I'm not. I want to leave, right now."

"Jo, we've discussed that."

"I don't mean run, I mean I want to get away from this police station. I want to go home."

"Okay, let's go." Eddy steered her towards the parking lot.

As soon as they were in the car Eddy started the engine.

"He thinks it was me, Eddy. I don't think he's even considering other suspects."

"Don't worry, pretty soon we're going to have plenty to give him to consider. Chris sent me a list of people to look into, all we have to do is narrow it down. I've already forwarded it to Samantha."

"Okay." She breathed a sigh of relief, but her heart still raced.

When they reached Samantha's villa, she was eager to find out who was on the list of people.

"Jo." Samantha smiled the moment she walked in. "I'm glad that it didn't go too badly this morning."

"Me too. Now, tell me that we have a better suspect than me." She pulled a chair up to Samantha's computer. Eddy sat down on the couch not far from them.

"I wish I could." She frowned. "Let me start with the bad news. We have a problem with our main suspect." Samantha pointed to a picture of David on the monitor.

"What is it?" Jo leaned close.

"He has an alibi. Walt told me he had paid a restaurant with his credit card on the day of the murder. At the time of the murder he was at a restaurant, alone, eating dinner."

"Maybe that's just his cover. Is it close enough to the gallery for him to slip out and kill Bruce then get back in time for his meal?"

"No. The restaurant is about an hour away from the gallery, and I've checked with the wait staff they remember him because his order was outlandish. He ordered the highest priced entrée on the menu and then demanded that it be sent back and cooked again. Trust me, the wait staff remembered him."

"So, a man who is facing financial ruin went out for a very expensive dinner while his partner was being murdered. It sounds to me like he knew something was going to happen and wanted to create an alibi for himself."

"It's possible that he hired someone to do the job, but we don't have any proof of that. This explains why the police might not even be considering him as a viable suspect. With an alibi this airtight there's no reason to keep him on the list."

"Which makes me the main suspect." Jo shook her head. "There's no one else for them to even look at."

"So far. But we have a few other options on our list."

"Oh?"

"This is Lou Conner." Samantha pulled up a picture on the monitor. "He runs another gallery in town that has been losing money so fast it's a wonder the doors are still open. The gallery took a nosedive after Bruce and David's opened. It's possible he was looking for revenge."

"Or trying to make a profit from stealing paintings from Bruce's gallery to sell on the black market." Jo snapped her fingers. "That causes Bruce's gallery to take a hit while boosting his own profits."

"Yes, that is also possible," Samantha said.

"Let's go have a conversation with Lou." Jo started to stand up.

"No, that's not a good idea." Eddy placed his

hand on her shoulder. "You need to keep a low profile and rubbing elbows with other suspects is not going to do that. Samantha and I will go talk to Lou. Is that okay with you, Samantha?"

"Sure, that's fine with me." She grabbed her purse from the table. "Jo, stay here while we're gone."

"I can go back to my villa."

"I'd feel more comfortable if you were here. We still don't know whether the person who killed Bruce might come after you," Eddy said.

"All right, but I don't need a babysitter."

"Good, because we're going to need Walt, too." Eddy pulled out his cell phone to give Walt a call as he and Samantha walked out the door. Alone in Samantha's villa Jo tried not to think about what the next few days might hold for her. If they didn't find a viable suspect to throw the attention off her she might be faced with the reality of an arrest and a trial.

Chapter Nine

Eddy drove from Samantha's villa to Walt's to pick him up. The scenic foliage that surrounded the road was lost on him, all of his focus was on how to keep Jo out of prison. Walt stood on the front porch ready to go as soon as Eddy arrived. He nodded to Samantha then climbed into the back seat.

"I'm not sure what you think I can do to help, but I'm willing to do anything that you ask."

"Good, because what we need you to do is give us a little class." Eddy smiled.

"I'm sorry?"

Eddy looked in the rearview mirror at him. "I know nothing about paintings."

"I know a little, but not as much as you." Samantha turned in her seat to look at him. "We think that Lou might have been stealing the paintings to sell on the black market. If that's the case he might have some of them in his gallery and we need you to be familiar with them in case they are. I've e-mailed you a list of the paintings that Bruce said were stolen from the gallery."

"I'll take a look."

As Walt searched the names of the paintings and studied the images, Eddy and Samantha discussed their approach.

"It's best not to tip him off that we are investigating. As far as he knows, you and I are looking for a new painting to hang above our mantle."

"Our mantle?" Samantha grinned. "Does that mean we're married?"

"I suppose." Eddy glanced over at her. "No need to go into detail. The important thing is that he will be at ease and think he's going to make a rare sale. That will give Walt time to look around at the paintings."

"If we're married, then who is Walt?"

"Our, butler?"

"Butler!" Walt sat forward in the back seat. "There's no chance of that."

"So we're married, and rich. I like this little fantasy, I think." Samantha laughed.

"Don't get used to it." Eddy winked at her. "We'll be lucky if we can pull it off."

"I am not going to be the butler."

"Okay, how about my brother-in-law? Samantha is your sister, you're close and you're helping us choose a painting."

"Fair enough." Walt nodded.

Eddy parked right in front of the gallery and the three climbed out to take a look around.

"Do you see how faded the sign is?" Eddy pointed out the sign that hung over the store front.

"And that front window is in dire need of a good scrub." Walt scrunched up his nose. "I hope it's not this dirty inside."

"Lou's definitely living on borrowed time."

Samantha stepped through the door of the gallery, with Walt and Eddy right behind her. "Oh, what is that?" She tucked a finger under her nose for a moment as her stomach swirled in reaction to a very strong scent.

"Bleach." Walt cringed.

"Well, you did hope it would be clean." Eddy smiled at him.

"I did, but that is very strong."

"Hello?" Samantha walked further into the gallery. "Is anyone in?"

"Just a minute!" A gruff voice barked from behind a door marked restroom.

"There aren't many paintings on the wall." Walt began to walk around the small gallery.

"Maybe he is trying to sell off what's left of his inventory." Samantha studied the paintings on the wall.

"That's right, which means you can get a great discount. See anything you like?" Lou stepped out of the bathroom and the scent of bleach followed him. "Sorry, I was just cleaning."

"No problem." Eddy locked eyes with him. "My wife and I are looking for a painting for our living room. Her brother's got a little experience in these matters."

"I see." Lou nodded and looked over at Walt. "See anything you like?"

"There's not much to choose from. What happened to the rest of your paintings?"

"I've sold them, and I don't intend to buy more. I just want to shut the place down."

"That's a shame. I would love to be surrounded by such beautiful art all of the time." Samantha lingered in front of one of the paintings.

"Look, I just opened the business because there weren't any other galleries in the area. Now there are and I can't compete. So once I get rid of what I have I'm shutting the doors. It's a disappointment, but you'll benefit from it. You can't beat close-out prices."

"You're right about that." Samantha smiled. "I'll see if there's anything that catches my eye." As Walt and Samantha began to walk around the gallery Eddy remained close to Lou.

"Tough business, huh?"

"It's tough, especially when you're in competition with criminals."

"Oh?" He raised an eyebrow. "What do you mean? Aggressive sales or something?"

"No, I mean real criminals. They steal the art, then sell the art. Pure profit."

"And they get away with this?"

"Well, I can't prove it, but I know that something isn't right. Anyway, it's not my problem anymore. I'm ready to start a new business."

"It's good that you can land on your feet like that."

"I made sure I had some money socked away

in case the gallery failed. Otherwise I'd be out of luck."

"This other gallery that you mentioned, do you know the owner?"

"No not personally, I've only heard about him. I heard that something bad went down there though."

"Like what?" Eddy shifted from one foot to the other and moved closer to the man.

"A murder. I don't know who yet, but I saw some posts about it on social media this morning. Like I said, criminals. The gallery is run by a bunch of thieves, and they have to face the danger that comes with that."

"You don't sound too sympathetic."

"I'm not. It's bad guys killing bad guys. Nothing to grieve about." He shrugged.

"Still, he could have been a good guy. Maybe he changed his ways."

"If he did, then why is he dead?" Lou locked

eyes with him. "Regular guys like us, we know what it's like to work hard to earn an honest living. Men like that, all they know is how to cheat and con people."

"What if it was the owner of the gallery that was dead? Would you keep this place open with your competition gone?" Eddy searched his eyes.

"No. It doesn't change anything. I'm tired of seeing the snobs that glide through here. They think they're something great and want to prove it with the right painting on their wall. It disgusts me."

"Well, that's no way to sell paintings." Eddy chuckled. "After all, I am here to buy one."

"You're not like these people though. Maybe your brother-in-law is a little bit, but not you, I can tell. You've been in the trenches."

"I guess you have been, too." He glanced up as Samantha walked towards him. "Did you find anything you like, darling?"

"No, I'm afraid not." She sighed. "We're going

to have to go to another gallery."

"Nothing?" Lou shook his head. "I know there's not much left to choose from."

"What you have are some quality paintings." Walt paused beside the three of them. "However, my sister's taste is a bit more modern."

"Understood." Lou nodded his head towards the door. "Good luck in your search."

"Thanks Lou." Eddy held out his hand to him. "Sorry we couldn't help you out."

"Don't be. Like I said, I'm closing either way." He shook Eddy's hand. As they walked out of the gallery Samantha leaned close to him.

"Did you find out anything?"

"I don't think he's our guy. But he knew that Bruce and his partner were criminals and believed they still are. That might be something to go on."

"What makes you think it wasn't him?" Walt settled in the car. Eddy pulled open the driver's side door.

"He's bitter, that's for sure, but he acted like he was going to close either way. What motivation would he have to kill Bruce?"

"Maybe he just didn't like the guy." Samantha buckled her seatbelt.

"He didn't seem to know him well. He also didn't seem to have much of a temper. I think we should put him on the back burner."

"All right, but I'm sure that's not what Jo is going to want to hear," Samantha said.

"I'm sure you're right." Eddy sighed as he drove out of the gallery parking lot.

Chapter Ten

Jo stopped pacing and stared hard at the wall. She couldn't let her friends do all of the work. They didn't understand the type of people that they were dealing with. She had a connection with most of the people they were meeting with. In fact, she was sure that if she saw David face to face he wouldn't be able to lie to her as easily as he would be able to lie to the police. Without thinking much more about it she grabbed her purse and headed out the door. She'd looked up all of David's information when she began to investigate him. She knew where he lived. If she got a look inside his house she might be able to figure out whether he stored the stolen paintings there. Even if he wasn't the killer, she was sure that he was still a thief.

Jo got into her car and drove towards David's house. She turned off the main street and parked a few blocks away from his house so that he wouldn't notice her car. He might have seen her the night that Bruce died, he might have killed Bruce. He might have known about everything.

Jo locked her car and walked down the street to the house. She noticed that there was no car in the driveway. As she approached the house she glanced around for neighbors. Nobody watering the lawn, and nobody walking their dog. Once she thought it was safe she knocked on the door. Satisfied that no one was going to answer it, she went to work picking the lock. She hunched forward to hide what she was doing. A moment later the door opened. Only, she hadn't turned the knob yet. Her stomach twisted as David stared at her with only an inch of space between them.

"Jo, I thought I'd be seeing you soon." He looked down at the tools that she still clasped tightly in her hands. "You don't have to break in. You're welcome to come inside." He took a step back and held the door open for her. She stared past him into the neat living room. She hesitated. It was a risk to be alone with the man she believed might have murdered Bruce. But if he was going to kill her, wouldn't he have already?

"Maybe we should talk out here."

"You don't have to be afraid, Jo." He smiled. "I'm not going to hurt you. I know why you're here. You want to know if I killed Bruce, right? Or if I'm going to kill you next?"

She searched his eyes. The David she'd met in the past was an intelligent man that wanted nothing to do with her. His only focus was the job. As far as she knew he wasn't close to anyone. Bruce had only met him shortly before she was arrested.

"I just want the truth, David."

"Then come inside. I'm not going to hurt you." He waited with the door held wide open. Jo took a breath and braced herself, then she stepped inside. He closed the door behind her. "I'm glad you stopped by, to be honest. I've been wanting to meet with you, but I wasn't sure how to do that without implicating myself, since, as you probably know, you're the main suspect."

"Did you kill him? Did you kill Bruce?" She studied him.

"I couldn't have. As I'm sure you already know I was out to dinner the night that Bruce was killed. I had nothing to do with his murder."

"Okay fine. Maybe you didn't, but maybe you know who did." Jo studied him for a moment. She didn't know him well, but she guessed that if Bruce trusted him enough to open a business with him there had to be a reason for that trust. "Don't you want to know who murdered him?"

"Of course I do." He narrowed his eyes. "I'm not convinced it wasn't you."

"I wouldn't hurt Bruce." She crossed her arms. "He saved my life once."

"Oh, I know. He told the story a million times. He was so enamored with Jo, the thief, as if you were some kind of superhero. But you never bothered to lift a finger to help him or repay him, did you?"

"I was in jail. When he needed help I offered it. Now, I am the main suspect in his murder. What else did you expect me to do?"

"I think that you had plenty of motive to go after Bruce. He was someone from your past that could out you."

"And I think that you had plenty of motive to go after Bruce, after all, he asked me to prove that you were stealing from the gallery."

David's face grew pale as he stared at her.

"He would never believe that. That's not true."

"It is. He wanted me to get proof that you were stealing the paintings because he didn't want to accuse you without it. That's what he asked for help with. That's why I was at the gallery when he was killed. I was waiting for you to sneak in to steal some more paintings."

"He died thinking I was stealing from him?" David lowered his eyes and clenched his jaw.

"David, whatever was between you and Bruce is your business, but I want to find out who killed

Bruce and make sure that they are locked up. Bruce wasn't a bad man."

"No he wasn't." He looked up at her again. "He was my best friend, and I would never do anything to harm a hair on his head. You can believe what you want about me, but nothing is going to change the fact that when he died, I was at a restaurant."

"Alone. Where was your girlfriend?"

"My what?" His cheeks flushed.

"Your girlfriend, who you spend all of your money on despite your financial troubles?" She looked into his eyes. "I happen to know about your excursions to expensive jewelry stores and women's clothing shops. I don't think you're the one that's wearing all of that, so why weren't you at dinner with your girlfriend?"

"I don't have a girlfriend. I have a few women I see off and on, and yes I do like to spoil them. There's nothing wrong with that."

"I guess not, if you don't mind bankruptcy,

but that's not my question. If you have a few girlfriends that you see why were you alone at the restaurant?"

"Because I had a meeting that fell through."

"A meeting with who?"

"Bruce was supposed to meet me at a gallery near the restaurant. It's owned by Robert Plathe. He was interested in selling us some paintings for the gallery. I showed up there and the gallery was closed, no sign of Bruce or Robert. After waiting for them for a while, I headed to the nearby restaurant. I was hungry. Is that a crime?"

"So you were supposed to meet with Bruce the night he was killed, but didn't bother to check on him when he didn't show up?"

"I thought I had my night and time wrong. Or that Bruce had intentionally told me the wrong night and time. He'd been leaving me out of things like that lately. Now I know why. I can't believe he thought that I was stealing from him. What a terrible thing to think." He clenched his jaw again and his hands balled into fists at his sides. "If only he'd just asked me instead of going behind my back, I could have told him the truth."

"Who do you think killed him, David? Other than me, obviously. Was he having any difficulty with anyone? Did you notice him arguing with anyone?"

"No. Nothing like that. Bruce went out of his way to be good to people. He said it was his way of repaying his debt to society. He didn't just start a new life on the straight and narrow, he wanted to be a good person." His cheeks flushed again as he looked away from her. "I wish I'd had the chance to learn more from him. I'm sorry I don't have more to tell you, but I just don't know anything else. As far as I knew everything was fine with Bruce. I have no idea why he was killed, but I had nothing to do with it."

"What about a guy named Lou who runs another gallery?"

"Lou? He wasn't too happy about us opening

the gallery, but we never heard from him again after that."

"His business is losing a lot of money and he is closing his gallery."

"Maybe he'd have motive then. I guess." He shrugged. "I don't know the man at all. I didn't do this, Jo, you must believe me?"

"I don't know what to believe, David. I think it's possible that you hired someone to kill Bruce. Then made a spectacle of yourself at a restaurant to ensure that you had an alibi. Is that what happened?" Her gaze pierced into his.

"No, it's not. Even if I wanted to hire someone, which I didn't, I don't have the money for something like that. You said yourself I have financial problems. I'm a compulsive spender, and I like the attention that women give me when I can spoil them. I've been trying to sell my personal things off so I have some cash to spend."

"Maybe you suspected that Bruce was on to you about the paintings and you knew that you weren't going to get to live your lifestyle for much longer. The easy solution would be to murder him, and then you could continue collecting the insurance on the stolen paintings."

"Keep quiet." David scowled as he crossed the short distance between them. "Don't you ever accuse me again!"

"Or what?" She refused to move an inch as she stared back at him. "I'm not afraid of you, David. All I want is the truth."

"Well, you're not going to get it from me, because I don't know it. I wish I did, but I have no idea what happened in the gallery that night. I don't know why Bruce believed I was stealing from him, but I wasn't." He closed his eyes and shook his head. "I have nothing else to say to you. Please, just go."

"I'll go. But if you think of anything that might give me a clue as to what happened to Bruce, you should call me. If you cared about Bruce as much as you say, then you should be interested in his murderer being found." She pulled out a card with her number and name on it from her purse and scribbled Eddy's number on the back of it. "If for any reason you can't reach me, call this number, he'll be able to get in touch with me."

"All right." He took the card from her and stared down at it. "So, you're on the straight and narrow now." He shook his head. "That's quite a change of pace."

"I have a different life now, I am a different person, David."

He scrutinized her, then nodded. "I'll call if I think of anything."

As Jo walked away from the house, her mind churned with thoughts of how David might have set up the entire murder. Clearly he had a reason to want to kill Bruce, but his alibi was airtight. She wondered if Robert might be the key. If he was really supposed to meet with Bruce and David, then someone must have canceled the appointment. He might at least have more information to offer. Preoccupied by her thoughts she walked right past her car and continued down the street. It wasn't until she heard a light laugh and the call of her name that she even recognized how far she'd gone. She was at the intersection of the main road and David's street. A woman waved to her from a car, then pulled up beside her.

"Jo, it's you isn't it?" She parked her car and stepped out. It took Jo a moment to recognize her, but once she did it was a shock.

"Leela?" She stared at her as her breath caught in her throat.

"Jo." She offered a tight smile. "It's nice to see you again. Although, I wish it wasn't because of my husband's death."

"Bruce? I had no idea that you and Bruce were married." Jo's eyes widened. "I'm so sorry for your loss."

"Well, you weren't exactly invited to the wedding, were you?" She pursed her lips as she studied her. "Maybe if you hadn't gone to prison, it would have been you instead of me."

"Leela, no matter what you think I was never interested in Bruce that way. He loved you and I'm sorry that he's gone."

"Are you really?" She leaned closer to Jo and searched deep into her eyes. "Don't think I don't know that the police are looking into you as a suspect."

"Leela, you know better than that. I would never hurt Bruce."

"Maybe not back then, but now?" She shrugged. "I'm not so sure I know anything about you. Anyway, it doesn't matter. Even when the cops figure out who killed Bruce it won't matter. He's dead, and he's not coming back." She fished in her purse for a moment and pulled out a tissue. As she dabbed at her eyes Jo reached out to touch her free hand.

"I'm so sorry. Bruce asked for my help, and maybe if I had figured things out sooner, I could have saved him."

"Have you figured them out now?" She lowered the tissue and sniffled. "Do you know what happened to my husband?"

"I'm sorry, I don't, not yet. But as soon as I figure it out I will let you know."

"Maybe you'll do a better job than the police. You know how it is, they see a record and they couldn't care less about finding a felon's killer. They kept talking to me about his past, as if that was the reason that he was dead. But, he was a changed man."

"Yes, I understand what you mean. But I'm not going to let that happen to Bruce. I will make sure that his murderer sees justice."

"I hope that you can." She sighed and wiped at her eyes again. "I didn't mean to startle you. I've been trying to work up the nerve to talk to you. Every time you got out of the car I considered stopping you, but I chickened out."

"You've been following me?"

"Once I heard that you were a suspect, I had

to see you again. And look at you, you're just as beautiful as you always were."

"Leela, you should have come to me. Why didn't you?"

"I didn't know what you'd think of me after all of these years. We weren't exactly friends back then. I know you didn't kill Bruce, Jo. He talked about you all the time. He admired your work so much."

"I don't do that kind of work anymore, and I'm not proud of what I did."

"Maybe not, but he still admired you." She frowned and lowered her voice. "I think he was in love with you, Jo."

"Leela, that's not true. Bruce only ever loved you."

"It seemed that way, but he got a special look in his eyes when he talked about you. I guess that's why I was always so jealous of you. All of it seems so silly now. He's gone."

"There was no reason for you to be jealous. All

I ever wanted from Bruce was his friendship. Now, I'm going to give him mine, and make sure that his murder is solved."

"Good. You do that, Jo. If anyone can I'm sure it's you." She patted her arm. "Keep me up to date." She handed her a card from her purse with her name and phone number printed on it. Jo took it and tucked it into her wallet.

"I will. Try to stay strong, Leela."

"I'll try."

Jo walked back to her car with a heavy heart. It was impossible to ignore the heartbreak in Leela's eyes. They had been together for so long, and now he was gone. She got into her car with renewed determination to hunt down whoever it was that killed Bruce.

Chapter Eleven

When Eddy and Samantha returned to Samantha's villa, Eddy noticed right away that Jo wasn't there.

"I knew it, I knew she wouldn't stay put."

"Relax Eddy. I'm sure she's fine. I'll text her. And by the way if it were you in her situation you wouldn't be staying put either. Would you?" She eyed him for a moment then looked down at her phone so that she could text Jo.

"No, I wouldn't. But that's not the point."

"I think it is. She's a bit old to parent, Eddy. If she wants to look into things for herself she has every right to. If she wants to go for a walk alone at two in the morning and howl at the moon she has every right to."

"That's ridiculous. Do you know how much crime is committed between the hours of one and three in the morning? You'd be safer jumping into shark-infested waters." Eddy scoffed.

"I've taken walks at two in the morning plenty of times and I've never come to any harm because of it."

"Why didn't you just ask me to walk with you?"

"Maybe next time I will." She smiled as she looked into his eyes. "But only if you're going to howl at the moon with me."

"I could use a good howl." He nodded. "Maybe we should take another look at David."

"With David having an alibi I didn't see much reason to look into him, but I can."

"Don't bother." Jo closed the door behind her. "He didn't do it."

"How do you know?" Eddy turned to look at her.

"Because I just spent some time with him, and as much as I hate to admit it, I'm convinced that he didn't do it. At least, not with his own hand."

"You went to see him alone?" Eddy shook his head. "That was a bad idea."

"I found out something interesting." She raised an eyebrow. "I dare you to tell me it was a bad idea after I tell you this."

"What is it?"

"Apparently, on the night of the murder David was supposed to meet with Bruce and another gallery owner, Robert. He thought the meeting was at Robert's gallery, but no one showed up. So he treated himself to dinner."

"So, why is that interesting?" Eddy shrugged.

"Because on the night of the murder, it's possible that Robert was at the gallery with Bruce. Maybe he saw something, or heard something that might help us."

"Or maybe he's the reason that Bruce didn't show up for the meeting. He might have done it. I'd like to have an idea about the man before I head off to talk to him," Eddy said.

"Sure, I'll look into him now. Robert Plathe,

right?" Samantha began typing.

"Yes. See what you can dig up." Jo sat down in a chair not far from Samantha. "I also ran into Bruce's wife, Leela."

"Oh? How did you run into her?" Eddy sat down on the couch.

"Actually, she was following me. I didn't realize Bruce was married. Leela was his girlfriend back when we worked together."

"Interesting." Eddy pursed his lips. "Any chance she had a score to settle with her husband?"

"I don't think so. She seemed pretty broken up about everything."

"What about money?" Samantha looked up from the computer. "Did she stand to benefit from his death?"

"I guess we'll have to ask Walt about that." Jo frowned. "I'd hate to think that she did it, but you're right the spouse is always a suspect."

"I'll check in with Walt and see if he can find any information about who benefits from Bruce's death." Eddy began to type out a text. "Can you tell us what you remember about Leela?"

"She was a spitfire. She usually found the jobs for Bruce and sometimes she participated in them. Most of the time it was just Bruce. She could be ruthless when it came to making sure that Bruce didn't get caught."

"Ruthless?" Eddy set his phone down.

"I mean in a protective way. She was even more than a little harsh to me, because she saw me as a threat. Bruce wasn't shy about praising me, and I think it bothered her. I know it bothered her. I never meant to do anything to come between them."

"Well, they were still together, right?" Samantha glanced over her shoulder. "So it doesn't seem like anything came between them."

"Unless." Eddy frowned.

"Unless what?" Jo met his eyes.

"Unless, Bruce's death had nothing to do with the paintings being stolen, and everything to do with you."

"Me? What do you mean?"

"Well, Bruce was killed right after you agreed to help him. Maybe Leela was more jealous than you thought. She heard that Bruce was working with you again, and decided to kill him before he could betray her. People have killed for far less."

Jo's cheeks flushed. "No, that's not possible."

"Jo, just because you don't want it to be true, doesn't mean that it isn't. I think you need to consider Leela a suspect until we can clear her."

"I guess we should." She stared down at her hands and shook her head. "That would mean it's my fault. Anyway, I never should have agreed to help Bruce."

"We don't know that, Jo, and no matter what none of this is your fault." Samantha turned away from the computer for a moment. "Here, I found something. Robert graduated from an art school four years ago, but before that I don't see a lot of information about him. I can't find any record of him attending high school in any nearby areas."

"Maybe he moved from a different state," Eddy suggested.

"Maybe. He's definitely careful about what he shares on social media. Even now that I've found his accounts there isn't much on them to give me an idea of his past."

"He could just be a private person. People are much more careful on social media these days."

"I wonder if he has a past, just like Bruce, David, and you. Maybe that's why he keeps a low profile."

"It's possible. I don't see any records of arrests, but Chris will be able to look into that better than me. Jo, you've never heard his name before?" Eddy asked.

"Never." Jo shook her head. "Maybe he used a different name back then, though."

"Let's keep looking." Eddy glanced at his

phone. "Walt just texted me to let me know there was a sizable life insurance policy on Bruce. Leela is the only named beneficiary."

"Sounds like we have a new prime suspect." Samantha smiled. Then her smile faded. "Wait a minute, I just got a hit on the list I searched before of known associates of Bruce's. This guy looks like he could be a candidate for the crime. He and Bruce were involved in a few thefts together about thirty years ago."

"Who is it?" Jo frowned. "That's around the time that I worked with Bruce."

"His name is Trent Dodge." She glanced over her shoulder at Jo. "Have you heard of him?"

"Are you sure that's right?" Jo's hands curled tight around the back of Samantha's chair. "I thought he was in prison."

"Yes. He was released last week."

"That's him, that's who did it." She took a step back from the chair as the face of a man she hadn't thought about in years flashed on the screen. He didn't look much older. His hair was gray around the edges and his eyes were a little more hooded, but he still had that same wicked smirk.

"How do you know?" Samantha stood up from the chair. "Have you met him?"

"Yes, I have. Bruce got him sent to prison. Bruce made a deal with the police. Dodge did the time and rumor is that Bruce never gave him a dime from their profits."

"That sounds like motive to me. Plus, he just got out of prison. Do you think it would be hard for him to find Bruce?"

"No. It's not like Bruce was keeping a low profile. I'm sure Bruce still had some contact with people from his past that Dodge did, too. It was a fairly small and tight circle."

"Then it won't be hard for him to find you either." Samantha's cheeks grew red. "We need to make sure that you're safe."

"No, you don't need to worry about me. But we need to find some proof that gets Dodge behind bars. He's a very dangerous man."

"A killer?" Samantha locked eyes with her.

"I didn't think so when I was younger, but he threatened everyone in the circle when he was the only one who went to prison. As far as I know his intentions of getting revenge haven't changed over the years."

"I'll get Chris to tip off Detective Rowan to look into him." Eddy picked up his phone again.

"Don't bother, I'll handle this. I'll speak to the detective myself."

Jo was already out of the villa before Eddy could dial the first number on the phone.

"Jo!" He stood up just as the door swung shut behind her.

"Eddy, let her go. She needs to do this. This is all part of her letting go of her past."

"Or walking right into a nightmare! Am I really supposed to stand by and watch her be this reckless?"

Samantha looked into his eyes. "I'll tell you what, the first time she does something that you've never done, then you can speak up. I get that you're being valiant, but it's coming across as sexist. Jo is just as capable of keeping herself safe as you are. I am too. If you want her to believe that you trust her, you're going to have to see her as an equal."

"It's not that I don't, you know that, Samantha. It's that there are very few people that I care about in this world, and I would like to keep all of them alive and well."

"Aw, Eddy." She patted his cheek with a light touch. "We're not going anywhere."

"Yes, just make fun of me." He sighed.

"I'm not making fun of you. I feel the same way about you, Eddy. I'm sure Walt and Jo do, too. But that doesn't change the fact that you have to let Jo be who she is and handle this the best she can. Okay?"

"Okay, if you say so. I'm going to go have a

conversation with Robert Plathe."

Chapter Twelve

When Jo reached the police station it was quite busy. She waited for some time to get the attention of the desk sergeant. Her heart pounded with the desire to turn around and leave. What sense did it make to walk right into the grasp of the police when she was their prime suspect? Still, she couldn't risk Dodge being on the loose. She hoped that bringing the detective a better suspect might lessen his interest in her. When the desk sergeant finally called her up, she requested a meeting with Detective Rowan.

"He's a little busy at the moment."

"Just tell him who is asking and I'm sure he'll see me."

"All right, I'll give it a shot." The desk sergeant picked up a phone and pressed a button then waited. He gave Jo's name, then nodded. When he hung up the phone he pointed down the hall towards one of the interrogation rooms. She swallowed hard at the thought of going back into one of those rooms. She walked towards it, but did not go inside. A few minutes later she heard the heavy footsteps of Detective Rowan approaching. She looked up as he paused in front of her.

"Shall we go inside?" He started to open the door.

"No." She folded her arms.

"I thought you wanted to see me?"

"I do. But not in there. We can talk here."

He studied her for a moment then nodded. "All right, if that's what you want to do. It's not going to change the fact that I have some questions for you."

"I'm here to give you information, to help your investigation."

"A confession?"

"No." She narrowed her eyes. "As I said before, I had nothing to do with Bruce's murder. I wouldn't even be here except I want Bruce's death to be solved. I want the man who did this to be behind bars."

"Okay, we want the same thing. What information do you have for me?"

"I have reason to believe that Robert Plathe met with Bruce at the gallery before he was killed. He might have seen or heard something that can give you an idea of who was there. However, I am pretty certain I already know who it was. There's a man who was just released from prison. Trent Dodge. He goes by Dodge. He went to prison because of a deal Bruce made with the police. If he's out and Bruce is dead, then I bet he is the one who did it."

"Trent Dodge." He nodded. "And how did you find this out?"

"I'm trying to clear my name, Detective Rowan. I haven't done anything wrong, and I don't want to go back to prison. There's no reason for me to lie to you."

"And yet you started off this entire

investigation by lying to an officer. You can understand why I don't believe a word you say." He raised an eyebrow and leaned against the wall.

"Believe it or don't, there's nothing I can do to convince you. But this is the man you should be looking into."

"Do you know him?"

"Yes. We crossed paths in the distant past."

"And you think he could be a killer?"

"When I knew him he wasn't that ruthless, but I do know that he was furious with Bruce when he went to prison. Rumor was that he threatened several people including Bruce. Maybe he has changed and become violent."

"And you? Have you changed?"

She frowned and looked away from him. "That was a different life."

"So you keep saying, and yet your different life seems to be a big part of your present life. Maybe you came in to throw this guy under the bus because you're afraid that I'm going to arrest you."

"No, that's not it. If I didn't think that Trent could be the culprit, I wouldn't be here."

"If Trent is as dangerous as you say, aren't you worried about him coming after you?"

"Maybe." She frowned. "But I'm more concerned that he's going to get away with murder because you're too busy focusing on me."

"Are you trying to tell me how to do my job?" Detective Rowan laughed.

"No of course not. I just thought that you would like the information and I am trying to do everything I can to help clear my name."

"For your information, I already know about Trent Dodge. And you're not the only suspect that I'm focused on. I'm also aware that Bruce had a meeting with Robert Plathe at his gallery before he was killed. He's on camera entering and leaving the gallery before Bruce's death. So, unless you have any actual new information, thanks for the insight, and enjoy the rest of your day." He turned around and walked down the hallway.

Jo stared after him and wondered if she had misjudged him. Maybe she was the one who wasn't a good investigator. After all, she had no idea Bruce was even in the gallery, or that Robert met with him, all of which happened while she watched from the parking lot. It was a relief to know that the detective was already aware of and looking into Dodge. The subtle reminder that she could be in danger too made her leave the police station with a little more caution.

***

The city streets flicked by as Eddy drove down a highway towards Robert's gallery. His mind churned with a mixture of protective instincts and his desire to trust his friends. Perhaps if he'd had more friends as a younger man it would be easier. But his entire life was about solving crime when he was a police officer. He barely spent time with anyone outside of the police station.

Eddy parked and walked up to the gallery. It had glossy illuminated signs and a vast display window. When he stepped inside the walls were covered with paintings, far more than even Bruce's gallery had on display. From the expansive layout and the numerous paintings it appeared as if Robert's gallery was much more successful than Lou's, or Bruce's.

"Welcome." A tall man with a thick, brown mustache stepped around a counter to greet him. "How can I help you?"

"I'm looking for Robert Plathe, the owner."

"I am the owner." He held out his hand. "You've found me."

"Robert, I'm Eddy." He shook his hand, then released it. "I'm looking into the murder of a friend of mine. I thought you might be able to help me with that."

"A death? I'm sorry, I deal in paintings."

"I'm aware, so did he. It was Bruce Langhord."

"I don't know anything about that."

"According to David Right, Bruce's business partner, you were supposed to have had a meeting at your gallery with himself, you and Bruce. From what I understand, you had that meeting with Bruce at his gallery instead."

"And you think I was somehow involved in Bruce's murder?" He laughed. "The police have already cleared me. Yes, I stopped by the gallery for our meeting. I was there for about ten minutes, then Bruce said he had something he needed to take care of so I left before him, and met my girlfriend at the restaurant on the corner for a quick bite to eat."

"Were you bothered when he cut short the meeting?" Eddy looked into his eyes and attempted to gauge his honesty.

"Honestly, I was annoyed. I'd been trying to work out a deal with him and David, then he wanted to leave David out of it. It seemed to me that his business and his life were a mess and I wasn't sure if I really wanted to get involved with that after all."

"Did Bruce mention why he had to run off?"

"No. I didn't care much about it. I was glad to get some extra time with my girlfriend. The waiter saw me there and I have the receipt for dinner."

"Was anyone else around the gallery when you left?"

"I didn't see anyone. There was a car in the adjacent parking lot when I arrived and when I left, but I didn't see anyone else. Maybe whoever was in the car had something to do with it."

"You didn't see anyone else?"

"No, like I said, I left to go see my girlfriend. Now, if you don't mind, I have some very important matters to attend to."

"More important than the death of a friend?"

"He was not a friend, he was an associate, and if you want information about who killed him maybe you should look into his partner. He's as crooked as they come."

"Were you aware that paintings had gone missing from Bruce's gallery?"

"Sure, I was."

"You seem to have an abundance. Is business slow?"

"No, I just always have the best artwork available. People seek my gallery out because they know they will get quality paintings. I offered to show some of my paintings in Bruce's gallery as he needed the business, and I needed the space."

"I see. And did you ever transfer any of your paintings to Bruce's gallery?"

"No. Once I realized that he suspected his partner of stealing paintings from his own gallery there was no way I was going to allow any of my paintings into that place."

"Okay, thanks for the information and your time." Eddy tipped his hat to him.

"Sure, next time you're in the market for a

painting, you know where I am." He handed him a business card.

"Thanks." Eddy tucked it into his wallet.

Chapter Thirteen

On the drive back to Sage Gardens from the police station Jo watched the sidewalks for any sign of Dodge. Would he come after her? If he came after Bruce, he might. Even though she had nothing to do with him going to prison, Dodge knew her to be a friend of Bruce's and that might be enough for him to want revenge. She parked near the community center instead of near her villa. If Dodge was watching her place, he'd be thrown off if he didn't see her car parked there. As she walked towards her villa she noticed a figure walking towards her. To her relief, it was Walt.

"Jo, hi." Walt smiled as he walked up to her.

"Hi." She turned to look at him. "Were you looking for me?"

"No, just a happy coincidence I suppose. Unless of course, you were looking for me?"

"No. I just got back from the police station."

"Eddy told me about that fellow, Trent Dodge. Are you concerned about him?"

"Not really. Maybe just a little bit." She frowned. "I'm not sure if killing Bruce is going to satisfy him. He might come after me because I worked with Bruce. I doubt it, but who knows."

"It would probably be best if we discussed a plan, just in case." He smiled at her.

"My plan is to sleep with one eye open." She laughed.

"Or, you could stay with a friend, in the spare bedroom." He lifted one shoulder in a shrug. "With me."

"Really?" She smiled. "I wouldn't want to invade your fortress of tidiness." Although Jo felt like she could take care of herself she felt like the company. She also knew that safety came in numbers, and if Dodge knew that Walt had been helping her investigate the murder he might come after him as well.

"Nonsense. It would be a pleasure to tidy up

after you. Besides, your other options are Eddy, who will likely lock you in a cage of some kind, or Samantha, who will chat you ear off all night. Unless of course, you don't think I can keep you safe."

"No, I don't doubt that for a second, Walt. I appreciate the offer, and I accept. If you regret it, you can always send me packing to Samantha's."

"Not Eddy's?" He grinned.

"I picture Eddy's hospitality being somewhat undesirable." She laughed. "I'm sure it would make him just as uncomfortable to have me under his roof."

"Then it's settled. You can stay with me until we are sure that this Dodge fellow is off the streets."

"Or I end up behind bars."

"No." His tone grew firm. "Never that."

"I agree. I'll just go pack up a few of my things and meet you at your place. All right?"

"Yes, I'll make sure you have fresh sheets." He smiled at her as he turned away. Jo continued towards her villa. It seemed odd to bunk with Walt, but she did think he was the better choice compared to her two other friends. Samantha, as much as she loved her, would never let her rest with her questions, and Eddy was a bit too overprotective. As if her thoughts summoned him, she nearly bumped into him beside one of the picnic tables.

"Jo, there you are. I saw your car in the parking lot by the community center and couldn't find you anywhere."

"I'm sorry that I worried you. I parked it there to try to throw off Dodge, in case he comes looking for me."

"Because you gave the police his name?" Eddy frowned. "You shouldn't have gone in there without me. You know I would have gone with you if you just asked me."

"Yes, I'm sure that you would have, but I

didn't want you to, Eddy. I don't want any of you more involved than you already are. This is my problem to fix."

"No, it's our problem. We're here to help you, I'm here to help you."

"I get that, Eddy. But the more you get familiar with my past, the more you're going to change your mind about me. I'd like to handle this myself so that I can keep some things private." She frowned. "Can't you understand that?"

"I can, but I can't believe that you still think I would think less of you."

"It's nothing personal, Eddy, I know that. You've spent your life putting people like me in prison, why would I expect you to accept me as I am now?"

"I haven't spent my life putting people like you away in prison, Jo. You're a completely different person now. And who is to say that if I caught you then I would have put you away? Maybe I would have seen you for who you really are and done my best to help you turn your life around? Maybe the reason you ended up in prison isn't so much the choices you made as it is that you didn't have the right kind of friends."

"Let's not play that game, Eddy. I know what I did, and I did my time for it. I turned myself into the police so I could put that part of my life behind me. But you don't have to go through all of this with me. I would like that part of my life to stay in my past, and if you know every little detail about it, then it's not going to stay that way. Please just try to understand that this isn't me being ungrateful for your help. This is me trying to own up to my mistakes, and do what I can to make them right without dragging everyone I care about into it."

Eddy sighed and pulled off his hat. He ran his hand back through his hair and smoothed it back against his scalp. "That's the thing, Jo, we do care about you. I care about you, and this is not something that you should be going through alone, no matter what you tell yourself."

"I'm not alone. I have you if I need you, when I need you. Right now, I'm just trying to keep my focus on what's right. This guy from my past, he's not the kindest soul. He's unpredictable, violent, and very likely a murderer. I don't want any of you getting tangled up with him. Until he's behind bars, he's going to come after everyone that tries to put him there."

"Then let me stay with you, so that I'll know you're safe."

"That much I can agree to, only I already accepted Walt's offer. I'm just getting some things from my place, then I'm heading over to his. You should probably think about staying with Samantha so that none of us are alone, just in case."

"That's a good idea." He nodded. "I'm sorry for being so heavy-handed about this. When it comes to these kinds of things I like to be in control."

"I know that." She laughed. "Unfortunately,

so do I. One of us has to give."

"You're right, it's your past, and your life. I will help you in any way that I can, but I will also do my best to respect your privacy."

"Thank you for that, Eddy, it means more to me than you realize."

"I'll be at Samantha's if you need me." He turned and walked back towards Samantha's villa. Jo walked up the path to her villa to pack a bag. Once she had a few things tucked into her bag she locked up the villa and began down the long path towards Walt's villa. The sunset had begun and splayed the world around her with rich oranges and pinks. She admired the sight with the same reverence she paid it after being released from prison. It was simple things like sunsets and walks in the park that she missed the most while she did her time. Her heart fluttered at the idea of losing those things again. She pushed the fear down, determined to have a positive attitude.

"Come over here, Jo!" She froze as the voice

seeped into all of her senses. She knew it, but she didn't want to admit it. She forced her feet to shift enough that she could turn towards the voice. His shoulders rested against the thick trunk of a tree. The gray flecks in his hair stood out to her against his pale skin. Her heart began to race the moment she locked eyes with him. "Come here!"

"No." Jo took a step back and stared at him with wide eyes.

"Don't act like a deer in headlights, you know who I am, I know who you are. Come here."

"No." She shook her head again, then glanced over her shoulder to see if anyone else was nearby.

"You know better than that, I'm not going to come anywhere near you when someone is around to see. I came here for a simple conversation, but I don't want us to have to shout to each other. If you won't come to me, then I'm going to have to come to you." He walked around the garden fence and moved towards her.

Jo's heart raced as she tried to decide what to

do. She could run inside, but that would only isolate her more. She could scream for help, but what if someone came running and was injured or killed because of it?

"What do you want, Dodge?"

"You know what I want. You gave the cops my name didn't you? You've got yourself a cozy little life here, but you couldn't let me have the same?"

"I didn't give anyone your name."

"Don't you lie to me." He growled his words and took another step towards her. "You know the entire time I was in jail it was because of Bruce and he got off scot-free."

"That had nothing to do with me." She narrowed her eyes. "What do you want, Dodge?"

"I want you to help me. The cops are going to come down on me hard for this. They're going to send me back to prison without even thinking twice. I want you to make sure that doesn't happen."

"How do you think I can do that?"

"I know you're friends with that retired cop. I've heard that he's doing his best to keep you out of prison. I want him to do the same for me."

"Dodge, Eddy's my friend that's why he's helping me. He knows that I didn't kill Bruce."

"And you think I did?"

"I think you could have. It's pretty obvious that you held a grudge against him for your time in prison. So why would it surprise me if you had something to do with his death?"

"Because I'm not a killer." He looked into her eyes. "You know that."

"I don't know anything. I do know that prison is hard, and it can change a person. Even if I didn't think you were a killer before you went to prison, I have no idea what you might be capable of now. Clearly you think it's okay to sneak up on someone in their own backyard, in the dark, and threaten them."

"I didn't threaten you, I just wanted to talk. But I see now that you really have changed. You think you're better than me because you have friends in high places. I know that's not the case. You don't want to help me? Fine, but I am not going down easy. There's plenty I can say that will implicate you."

"Even if you do that won't make a difference. I had no motive to hurt Bruce, but you did."

"I didn't kill him. Was I angry at him? Sure, but I didn't kill him. Maybe Bruce threatened to out you to your new friends? I bet they wouldn't like that too much."

"I doubt they would care. My friends know about my past and they still accept me."

"That's what you think now. After they hear my spin on it, they might not feel the same way."

"I doubt that. You can threaten me all you want, but it's not going to change the fact that you're the best suspect."

"All right." He frowned. "You're right. We're both on the line here, and you claim you're innocent, I know that I'm innocent. I just need to prove it."

"Are you asking for my help?"

"No, forget it. I'll be fine." He waved his hand at her then walked off in the other direction. She stared after him and wondered if she should stop him. If he was the killer she might be able to get more information out of him, but she could also put herself in a very precarious position. If Dodge believed she had something to prove he was the murderer, he might not hesitate to kill her to keep her quiet. From now on she had to be more careful.

Chapter Fourteen

By the time Jo reached Walt's villa she had goosebumps all over her skin. Walt stepped outside to greet her, but the moment he saw her, his smile faded.

"Jo, what's happened?" He guided her inside the house. "Are you okay?"

"It's nothing, I'm fine. I just want to get inside."

"It's not nothing, you're shaking." He closed the door behind them and turned the lock. "What happened?"

"I ran into Dodge on the way back from my place. He claims he had nothing to do with Bruce's death, but just being near him made my skin crawl."

"Should we call Detective Rowan and let him know what happened?"

"No, I've had enough of him today. I just need

to relax a little bit I think."

"I have the perfect thing for that. Just sit down for a moment and I'll have it ready for you, all right?"

"That sounds good." She sat down on the couch and breathed a heavy sigh. What was she going to do about Dodge? If Detective Rowan didn't take him seriously then he might not be arrested. The idea of him roaming around free made her uneasy. The whistle of the kettle cleared her thoughts just before Walt took it off the burner. She smiled at the thought of the warm tea that would soon settle her nerves. Would it be enough to calm her? Maybe not, but it couldn't hurt.

"Why don't we take these out on the back porch. The sunset is fast approaching."

"Yes, that sounds nice." She stood and followed him onto the porch.

"Here you go, chamomile for you, and mint for me." He handed her a mug, then sat down in the chair beside her. "Something to warm the soul."

"Do you believe in that?" She took a sip of her tea. "Thank you for this."

"Souls? I'm not sure. I hadn't really thought much about it."

"I would have assumed that someone like you would already know exactly what he thought about the supernatural."

"Honestly, it never drew my interest. I like the idea that there might be something special out there that would connect all of us, but that's just a wish. There is nothing in science at this time that points to that."

"I see." She gazed out at the water that the porch faced. "I wonder sometimes if we're missing out on something though. I mean, isn't it strange that someone from my past showed up, and is gone the next day? Doesn't that have to mean something?"

"I suppose it could. But you have to factor in

that you and your acquaintances from your previous life were involved in high risk jobs, so it's much more likely that one of you would end up dead."

"Thanks." She shook her head and set down her mug. "I guess I needed to know that."

"I'm sorry." He sighed and set down his mug as well. "I'm not good at comforting. I never have been. It's so much easier to hide behind facts and trivia than it is to talk about real emotions. You've lost a friend, and that's not something I should be so detached about."

"It's all right, Walt. You don't have to be good at comforting. You're good at so much more than that. Besides, you make a good point. Bruce was involved with the wrong people and that was enough to get him killed."

"Are you still thinking it was David?"

"Honestly, I don't know anymore. With Dodge in town, it could have easily been him from what he said. I don't think he has an alibi. I just want one shred of proof that will point in the right direction. Does that seem like too much to ask for?"

"Not at all, but finding it is not going to be easy. Too many times we try to take the obvious and easy road, that's why the investigation has to focus quite a bit on you. You're the obvious suspect." He picked up his tea again and took a sip. Jo watched him for a moment, then looked into his eyes.

"You know I didn't do this, right? I mean, it's okay if you thought that I might have, I just want you to know that I absolutely did not."

"I don't doubt that for a second. you're not a killer, Jo, and you never will be. No matter what you might get caught up in, I know that it's not your fault."

"Isn't it though?" She looked back out at the water. "I keep telling myself that if I didn't offer to help him, none of this would have happened."

"I would venture to guess that whoever killed

Bruce would have still killed him, and the main difference would be that he wouldn't have a dedicated, skilled friend looking into his death."

"That may be true, but I also wouldn't be the main suspect in his death. Still, you are right. I am glad that I am able to be involved in the investigation, and that I have such good friends to help me through it."

"And we will, in every way that we can."

"You have no idea how much I appreciate that." She took a sip of her tea and began to rock the rocking chair.

"You know, in all of this, we're forgetting something."

"What's that?" She swirled the tea in her mug.

"You lost a friend. Maybe you didn't know Bruce that well anymore, but there was a time when he was an important part of your life. He had to be, otherwise you wouldn't have helped him."

"Yes, you're right about that. He was someone

I admired. I guess in some ways I considered him a teacher."

"I know you've mentioned that he saved your life. How did that happen?"

She shifted in her chair and glanced over at him. "Is that something that you really want to hear about?"

"Yes, it is. I'd love to know more about you, Jo, all of you, including your past. If this man protected you, then I would have liked the chance to thank him."

"That's nice of you, Walt." She took a sip of her tea. "It was a high end job, a break-in at a mansion to retrieve two small paintings. It was at the beginning of my career and there was more than one painting so we teamed up. It made it easier, and although we would split the profits, there was less chance of coming out with none. So, Bruce and I teamed up for this particular job. It was the only job I worked on with another thief. Too many complications when you have to rely on someone else. But lucky he was there on this job. There was more intense security than we expected. Bruce was halfway out a window when he noticed I was caught in the middle of the living room. The man who owned the mansion had rigged the alarm system so that if someone set foot on the carpet in the living room it would go off. It wasn't a matter of waiting for the police to arrive, the homeowners had their own private security that was never more than two minutes away. That still would have been enough time for me to escape, except that I got my foot wedged under the couch. I was a sitting duck, and Bruce had both of the paintings. He could have just left, let me take the fall, and never looked back. Instead he chose to help me. We got out of the home, and were in the street when the security guard started firing on us. Bruce pushed me out of the way of a bullet and took one in his arm. We managed to escape, but if he hadn't pushed me I don't think I would still be here."

"It sounds like he cared about you."

"Yes, maybe too much. His girlfriend didn't like it."

"And you? How did you feel about him?"

"I was a different person then." She gazed into space. "I didn't think I needed anyone. I didn't want anyone. I pushed everyone away. But I did want to learn from him and he wanted to teach me. I realized how much he cared about me the day he risked his life and freedom for me. But then we went our separate ways and we had very little contact with each other. I preferred to work alone. Then I turned myself in. I went to prison. He did send a letter to me in jail explaining how he had changed, but the first time I had contact with him in person since I was arrested was the other day."

"Did you ever miss him?"

"Not really. We weren't that close and I let go of that life. I knew I needed to focus on where I was, and how to change my life going forward. I guess I cut off all of my connection to that life."

"Still, it must be hard to know that he's gone."

"Hard, yes. But I wouldn't have invited him back into my life as a friend. I planned to do him this one favor because I owed him. But then I planned to move on from there. You can see how well that worked out."

"I'm sure it's not what you expected."

"To be honest, when I ran into him, I was surprised that he was still alive. I thought he would have done something risky years ago. Now I find out that he's married to his then girlfriend, and I realize he had an entire life while I was behind bars. A life that I was not part of, and a life that in many ways I didn't get to have."

"It seems a bit romantic to me that two people involved in a criminal life could change together and start a new way of life. You don't see that happen too often."

"It is surprising. Especially since Leela was always so engaged in the lifestyle. If anything Bruce was more cautious than she was. He spoke about doing that one big job and then retiring from crime to enjoy his life. Leela was never like that. One big job, only meant that there could be another big job out there for her."

"Maybe something happened that scared her."

"Maybe."

"We'll figure it all out, Jo, you just relax, soak in those beautiful colors, and remember that soon all of this will be just a memory."

Jo followed his instructions and gazed out at the sky again. Peace washed through her body as she took a deep breath of the balmy air. If only life could be simple.

Chapter Fifteen

Early the next morning Eddy emerged from the bathroom to find Samantha at the coffee pot.

"Ready for your morning joe?"

"Sure, I could use it. I had a hard time sleeping last night."

"Oh, was the couch too lumpy?"

"No, it was fine. I'm just trying to get my head around things so that I can plan the next step in this investigation," Eddy said.

"I thought finding out about Leela was interesting. I know that Jo thinks that it's probably Dodge, but I'm not so sure. Would someone who just got out of prison really risk taking revenge so soon? Wouldn't his freedom be more important than an old grudge?"

"I don't know, it's hard to say. I've seen criminals that have brooded over a grudge for decades and still come after the person they felt was responsible," Eddy said.

"Yes, that may be true but don't you think more planning would go into that?"

"I'm not sure if more planning would or not. Maybe he wanted to confront Bruce, maybe he didn't plan to kill him at all, but maybe he arrived there and once he saw him he decided to go through with it."

"Okay, so where did he get the gun? He's been out of prison for a few days, could he really get one that fast?"

"Not legally, but I'm sure he still has some contacts on the black market that might be able to provide him with a weapon if he needed it. Maybe he even had one stashed away from before. It's not surprising to me that he would be armed."

"I suppose that makes sense," Samantha said.

"But what about the wife? Walt said she would profit the most from Bruce's death."

"It's definitely a possibility. I wonder how Jo is holding up."

"A bit like a caged animal. Walt's texted me a few times that she's restless. I've told him to keep a close eye on her to make sure she doesn't escape through the bathroom window."

"She would totally do that." Samantha laughed, but her amusement faded fast. "She has to be terrified of going to jail."

"Let's not think about that. Yes, she has good reason to be afraid, but it's not going to help anything if we are afraid, too," Eddy said.

Samantha looked up from the computer screen long enough to meet his eyes. "But you are aren't you? Afraid?"

Eddy narrowed his eyes and nodded. "Yes, I am. There is the possibility of a strong case against Jo. If we don't find something fast she might be arrested, and after that we're not going to be able to do much investigating of our own."

A knock on the front door drew both of their attention. Eddy shot a sidelong look in Samantha's direction.

"Be cautious."

"I will." She walked up to the door and peered through the peephole. A smile sprang to her lips as she saw who was on the other side. She opened the door and Jo stepped inside with Walt right behind her.

"Hi everyone, we brought breakfast." Jo held up a bag of bagels.

"Perfect timing, the coffee is fresh."

"You should really limit your consumption of caffeine." Walt wagged his finger in Samantha's direction.

"I'll stop drinking coffee, when you stop drinking tea, Walt." She winked at him.

"It's not the same thing."

"Maybe not, but that's when I'll stop. I'll get us some plates." As everyone assembled around the table to enjoy breakfast, Eddy rapped his hand lightly on the table.

"So, we're at a bit of a standstill." Eddy

frowned. "I think it's time we got an expert's advice on this."

"I've told you everything that I know." Jo spread her hands out in front of her.

"I'm not talking about you, Jo. I'm talking about someone who was more recently involved in crime, and knows the gallery very well."

"David?" Her eyes widened. "You want to ask for David's help?"

"Why not? He's the only person that we know for sure didn't kill Bruce."

"It's still possible that he hired someone to do it." Jo tapped her finger on the table.

"If he hired someone then he must have pulled the money from some hidden account, very well hidden." Walt shook his head. "As far as I could tell, David is broke."

"But I've already talked to David and he didn't have anything to tell me about the murder," Jo said.

"About the murder. But what about the stolen paintings?" Eddy looked between the three of them. "We've been so focused on the murder that we've forgotten about the reason for Jo helping out Bruce in the first place. Someone was getting in and out of the gallery without setting off the alarm or being recorded on the cameras. Bruce's murderer was able to do the same thing. So, we should be paying attention to the stolen paintings, too."

"That's a good point." Jo nodded. "It's not likely that two people managed to skirt such good security."

"And David is going to be the best one to advise us on how that skirting might be done, and whether anyone who seemed suspicious had been around the gallery," Eddy said.

"You're right." Samantha nodded.

"There's also Leela to consider. I think we need to find out more about her," Eddy said.

"We know she's got financial motive." Walt

nodded.

"But she was in love with Bruce. I find it hard to believe that she would have killed him. I know, I know, people have killed for less." Jo sighed. "I guess maybe I want to believe that they were in love until the end."

"There's nothing wrong with that, but we need some cold hard facts to move us forward. Let's start with David and see where it leads us. Is that okay with you, Jo?" Eddy looked over at her.

"Yes, I think that's the best place to start," Jo said. "But I am coming with you."

"I don't think that's a good idea," Eddy said.

"He will be much more forthcoming with information if I'm there," Jo said. "It's our best shot."

"Okay, but I don't like it." Eddy shook his head.

After they had finished breakfast they piled into Eddy's car and headed off to Bruce's gallery. When they drove up to it, Jo had to hold back a flutter of emotions. The last time she was there, she found Bruce dead. Strengthened by the presence of her friends, she walked into the gallery. David looked up from a desk positioned not far from the hanging paintings.

"Jo? It's a bit daring of you to come here." He stood up as they walked towards him. "Who is this, the cavalry?" He stared at the group of people before him.

"My friends. I guess you could call them that. We're here to ask for your help."

"My help?" He laughed. "I doubt that."

"It's true. We realized that you might be able to help us out with something."

"With what?" He stared hard at Jo. "Are you trying to get me to confess to a crime that I didn't commit, again?"

"No. I want to know how someone got into the gallery, without setting off the alarm or being recorded, to kill Bruce. The alarms and cameras were avoided when the paintings were stolen, too.

I saw how sensitive that alarm was when a couple of kids just touched the glass. So, that alarm had to be turned off in order for someone to get inside."

"You're right, it probably was."

"Then how did the thief, or the murderer get access to the alarm?"

David shook his head. "I've been trying to figure that out myself. I called the alarm company and they said that the alarm was working normally during those times. It had been disarmed using the codes. Only Bruce and I have the code."

"So, if Bruce went into the gallery he might have been the one to turn off the alarm."

"Yes, it's very likely that he did." David shrugged. "But why weren't the cameras rolling? That's something I can't tell you. I checked the DVD and there was nothing there. For some reason the footage stopped about fifteen minutes before Bruce was killed. After you told me about the missing paintings I went back through some of the old footage and found similar gaps in the recordings."

"Was there ever anyone that visited the gallery on the day that the footage was interrupted who stood out to you?" Eddy asked.

"No, I don't think so. It's hard to say, though, I can only tell who entered the gallery from the footage I saw."

Eddy rested his hands on the table and studied the man before him. "Why do you think your partner suspected you?"

"Are we really going to hash this out again? He probably suspected me because I've been short on cash lately. We also hadn't been getting along. I told him something about his wife that he took offense to."

"What did you tell him about Leela?" Samantha asked.

"She was at the gallery one night and her cell phone rang. Before she answered the call, she went outside. I thought this was a little strange so I followed her. Once she was outside she answered the phone and kept her voice down. I thought it was odd, but I let it go. Then it started happening just about every night she was here, and one time I overheard her call the person on the phone sweetie. Bruce was my friend, I didn't want him to be played by a woman. So I mentioned to him that he needed to keep an eye on her, that she might have a boyfriend. But he got angry at me and told me I was just trying to drive a wedge between them. I wouldn't do that. I like Leela. Maybe I shouldn't have said anything to him. Maybe I misunderstood the situation. After that he gave me the cold shoulder."

"Do you have any idea who Leela might be seeing?" Jo searched his eyes. "Someone from the past?"

"No, I don't know. Like I said, it was only those brief conversations that I knew about. I never saw her with anyone in particular."

"No one was hanging around? Making an

extra effort to see her?"

"No, after Bruce got mad about it, I stopped paying attention. It wasn't my business."

"Interesting. What about Dodge?" Jo watched his facial expression as she delivered the question. He froze, and stared hard at the papers on the desk.

"What about him?"

"Do you know him?"

"Yeah, I know of him."

"Has he been around?"

He walked around to the front of the desk and paused beside Jo.

"Maybe this is something to discuss in private."

"No. Anything you want to tell me, you can tell my friends, too."

"Fine. Yes, Dodge has been around. I didn't think he'd be much of a problem once I told him that we weren't interested in any jobs."

"Wait a minute, Dodge came here to ask you about working a job?"

"It was more like he came here to ask if we knew of any for him. I guess he was pretty desperate for money after getting out of prison." He shook his head. "I didn't really think much of it."

"Even though Bruce was the reason that Dodge went to prison?" Jo shoved her hands into her pockets. "You didn't think that was something to be concerned about?"

"From what Bruce told me. No. He'd been writing back and forth to Dodge in prison in an attempt to work things out. I think maybe he even offered Dodge a job, and maybe Dodge didn't realize it was an actual regular job."

"So they mended their friendship?" Samantha glanced over at Eddy then back at David. "Even after all of those years?"

"I wouldn't say mended. But Bruce was attempting to settle things with him. Help him out if he could."

"Was he afraid that when Dodge got out he would come after him?" Eddy nodded to Jo. "Or others?"

"Bruce didn't seem to be afraid. But then he didn't speak to Bruce. He spoke to me. When I told him that we weren't interested in any jobs, he got a little annoyed and took off, like I'd wasted his time."

"You should be careful," Eddy suggested. "Just because he walked away the first time, doesn't mean he won't come back for revenge."

"I know. I'm taking precautions."

"What about the cameras?" Walt glanced around the gallery at them. "Is there a way to disable them without disabling the alarm?"

"Yes, they're totally separate from each other. However, the only way to disable them is through the computer which you have to have a password for. Only Bruce and I knew the password. No one else could have tampered with it."

"I wouldn't say that. There are some people who are able to crack into any computer, even from their own computers. Maybe the system was hacked into from the outside." Samantha typed something on her phone. "I'll check with one of my contacts and see if there are any known hacks recently and whether there is some kind of program that will give someone else remote control access of the system."

"Good idea." Jo nodded. "David, thanks for your time."

"Sure. Anything I can do." He shook his head. "I'm still having a hard time believing that he's gone."

Jo's gaze lingered on him. Was he genuine? It was hard for her to tell. When they got back to the car, Eddy sat behind the wheel for some time.

"So, now we suspect that Leela was seeing someone else? That ups her as a suspect."

"Yes, it does." Jo squinted through the windshield at the gallery. "But we also know that

Dodge was hanging around here."

"Good point."

As they left the parking lot, Jo's cell phone began to ring. She stared down at her phone. The last person she expected to call her was Leela, and yet there was her number staring back up at her.

"Hello?"

"Hi Jo. I'm sorry to bother you. I was wondering if you might help me with something." Jo flashed back to her conversation with Bruce for a moment, then cleared her throat.

"Yes sure, what do you need?"

"I have to clean out the house. I want to get it on the market as soon as possible and I need to get the stuff ready for the movers. Is there any chance that you might want to help me with that? I know you are looking for some extra cash and I'm happy to pay you. You know, Bruce and I never had children and I don't have anyone to help me."

"Oh." Jo smiled a little. It would be a great

way to look through Bruce's possessions while also gauging the potential of Leela's involvement. "Of course I'll help, but there is no need to pay me. Do you want me to come right now?"

"Is that too much trouble?"

"No, I'm just out with some friends, I'll have them drop me off."

"Great, I'll be here, in the middle of a huge pile of mess."

"See you soon." She hung up the phone and looked into Eddy's inquisitive eyes. "I need you to drop me off at Bruce's house."

"Why?"

"Leela invited me, and I think it will be a great way to get some information about her while you follow up on the cameras, and the alarm company."

"Okay." Eddy nodded and turned the car in the right direction.

"Okay? That's it?"

"That's it. If you think it's the best course of action, then it is."

"Thanks Eddy."

Chapter Sixteen

After some time Eddy pulled the car up to a small house. The green paint on the outside had begun to peel. The porch itself was scattered with junk that should have been tossed out or placed in storage. A snow shovel still rested by the door despite the warm weather. It seemed to Jo that Bruce didn't do much to take care of the house.

"So, do you want Walt or Samantha to stay with you?"

"No, I think it's best that I do this by myself. She's not going to be as open around anyone else. I might just be able to get more information or even a confession out of her if I gain her trust."

"Keep in touch with us, okay?"

"I will." She glanced in the back seat at Samantha and Walt. "Text me if you find out anything about the security system, okay?"

"You've got it." Samantha reached forward to

pat her shoulder. "Be careful."

"I will be." She walked up to the door with heavy steps. Her entire body was weighed down by the notion of being inside Bruce's house. Would she be able to see past his loss and get some actual evidence of a crime? When she stepped onto the creaky porch, the front door swung open.

"Jo!" Leela smiled "I'm so glad that you could take the time to help me with this."

Jo offered her a warm smile. "I'd hate to think of you dealing with this alone." Leela led her inside the home. The piles of belongings scattered all over the living room startled her. Leela had been hard at work in the short time since Bruce's death.

"I know it's a wreck, I'm sorry. I'm trying to get this done as fast as possible. I want to leave all of this behind me."

"Just tell me what I can do to help, I'm here. I know this must be such a difficult task for you."

"It's not really. I've been dying to do this for years. Now, at least I get a fresh start." She sighed and looked around the living room. "Can you help me with this?" She picked up a stack of papers and pointed to a box in the corner. "I want to make sure everything is boxed up before the movers come."

"It seems rather fast for you to leave so soon. Are you sure you're giving yourself enough time to recover?"

"It seems fast, but it's not really. Bruce and I had always hoped to move, he just happened to die before we could do it. I'm not going to let another day of my life go by without getting to do what I hoped to. It all goes so very fast."

"Yes it does." Jo put the stack of papers into the box. As she did a receipt fluttered to the floor. She reached down to pick it up and recognized the name of the restaurant on the top of the receipt right away. It was for LaRuse. "Bruce, the romantic." She smiled as she looked over at Leela. "Did he take you to LaRuse often?"

"Bruce? Ha! That man wouldn't be caught dead in a fancy restaurant." She gulped and covered her mouth. "I probably shouldn't talk like that."

"I know what you meant, it's okay. But you two were getting along well, right?"

"As well as an old married couple can. We had our ups and downs over the years, of course. I certainly never expected to spend the later years of my life living in this shoe box in a nowhere town, but that's what he wanted, so." She shrugged.

"You didn't agree with him leaving the life?"

"It wasn't so much that. I mean we were both getting a bit old for it. But instead of investing all of our money in some beautiful place where no one would ever find us, he bought that gallery and opened it. He told me it was his chance to be a real businessman. I thought it was ridiculous, but my opinion didn't hold much weight." She wrapped a plate in newspaper. "I thought it was a phase that he would get bored with, but he really took to it. He was right, too, most of the people we met had no idea about our past. It was rather nice to be treated as if we were just regular people."

"I'm sure it was." Jo smiled. "I've enjoyed that myself."

"It's odd though, isn't it? Sometimes that old life, it just calls to you. The thrill, the money, the adventure, the money." She laughed. "I never knew what it was like to have to balance a checkbook before. All of that has changed now. I'm going to have to figure out the finances all on my own."

"Did Bruce take care of you?" Jo frowned. "Did he make sure you'd live well?"

"Oh yes, he had quite a life insurance policy, but that won't be paid out until the investigation is complete of course." She rolled her eyes. "I don't know why it matters who killed him, he's dead either way, isn't he?"

"Yes, yes he is." Jo paused in front of a

photograph of herself with Bruce and Leela. "I can't believe you've still got this."

"I can. Bruce always had a heart for you, Jo."

"I never forgot what he did for me, Leela. That's why I agreed to help him."

"Maybe you shouldn't have." She sighed and shook her head. "Maybe he was killed because he was looking into the wrong thing."

"I was very careful, Leela."

"I'm sure that you were, but we don't know who killed him, do we?" She sighed. "I guess we may never know. I can't wait to get as far from this house as I can possibly go. A new chapter awaits me."

"I'm sure it does." Jo turned back towards her. "Although, you'll need time to grieve as well."

"Yes, that's true. It'll be easier to do away from here though." She turned away to add another plate to her box. As she did Jo casually tucked the receipt for LaRuse that was still in her hand into her pocket. She wasn't sure why she was keeping it, but she knew she wanted to look at it more when Leela wasn't there to see her. Jo began to wrap the other plates so that she could help her along. Could Leela be right? Had she unwittingly alerted the wrong person to Bruce's knowledge that the paintings were stolen?

After a few hours, Jo sent a text out to her friends to see who might be willing to pick her up. As she waited outside for someone to show, she thought about the receipt in her pocket. It only took a few minutes for her to realize why she had put it in her pocket. Walt's car pulled up at the end of the driveway. She walked towards it, dazed by the connection she'd made.

"Ready?" Walt smiled at her as she climbed into the car. Jo couldn't smile back. Her heart still ached as she watched Bruce's house disappear. Maybe they would have been friends again, had they the chance. "Jo, you can talk to me about anything, you know that right?"

"Yes." She sighed. "I keep waiting for some kind of closure. But, I don't think solving the murder is going to give it to me."

"It's not that kind of closure." He nodded a little. "You need closure for your friendship."

"Was it even a friendship? Can you call someone that you live a criminal life with a friend?"

"Sure you can. He was there for you when you needed him. Yes, your lifestyle was different then, but his friendship was the same as mine. Loyal, and unwavering."

Jo looked over at him with a small smile. "You always know how to calm me down, Walt."

"Trust me, I've spent years calming myself down. It's easy to get caught up in the details of things, but when you get down to the core of any relationship, it's the same essential connection. Two people care for each other. That sounds simple, but in order for one human to care that much about another human there has to be more than just common interests, there has to be an instinctive connection. Kind of like how dogs sniff each other's bottoms."

"I'm sorry, you lost me at that last part?" Jo laughed.

"But you smiled didn't you?" He grinned. "Just like dogs sniff each other's bottoms, our instincts tell us when someone feels safe, or dangerous. Even in the middle of a very dangerous lifestyle your instincts told you that Bruce was safe, someone who genuinely cared about you. Honestly, we don't get many of those connections in our lives, so we deeply value the ones we find."

"That's it." Jo nodded and stared out through the windshield. "Even though he was involved in a life I wanted to leave behind, I still valued him. I still do. He helped me when I needed it."

"Then he was a good person, Jo." Walt patted her hand as it rested on her knee. "You don't have to be afraid to call him that." Jo bit into her bottom lip and remained silent as Walt turned the car into Sage Gardens. As he drove towards his villa he looked over at her again. "And so were you, Jo, no matter what you tell yourself, no matter what crimes you committed, you were and still are a good person."

"I have to go." Jo pushed the door open the moment the car stopped.

"Are you okay?"

"I'm fine. I just need a walk to clear my head." She stepped out of his car. "Thanks for the ride." She smiled at him and then turned away. She felt Walt's eyes on her as she walked away from his villa and towards the lake. What Walt had said to her struck a chord. Not once in her younger years did she consider herself a good person, but maybe that was why she lost herself so easily in criminal acts. When she reached the lake Jo slipped her shoes off and stuck her toes in the edge of the water. It was murky and cold, but the subtle ebb and flow against her skin made her relax and think clearly. A few minutes later she became aware of another presence. Her heartbeat quickened as she thought it might be Dodge.

However, when she looked over her shoulder she saw the three familiar faces of her friends.

"Sorry to interrupt." Walt rubbed her shoulder. "But you shouldn't have to be alone." Without another thought Jo turned to face Walt. He pulled her close. She rested her head against his shoulder.

"Thank you, Walt."

He kissed the top of her head, without worrying about germs, dandruff, or shampoo residue. "It's what friends do."

"I'm glad you're all here," Jo said as she pulled away from him. "I hope you can help me sort this out." She pulled the receipt from her pocket. "It's for the same restaurant that David visited with his unknown girlfriend. I'm not certain, but I think the dates are the same, too. Leela said Bruce never took her there. So who did?"

"Hm." Walt skimmed the receipt. "Yes, it's the same date, and for a similar amount. Maybe they split the bill?"

"You think that Leela was cheating on Bruce with David?" Jo asked.

"Maybe." Samantha took a look at the receipt. "David said that she was having an affair. He was so ready to throw Leela under the bus, maybe so that he could protect himself from suspicion."

"Then perhaps while David ate and gave himself an alibi, Leela was at the gallery ending her relationship with Bruce." Eddy rubbed his chin. "Maybe she decided that she wanted to be with David instead."

"If they were working together to steal the paintings and Bruce found out, then they might have both wanted to get rid of him." Jo sighed. "I hate to think it of Leela, but it's beginning to add up."

"So, if David was lying to us the entire time, we can't take anything he said as valid information." Samantha groaned. "We're back to square one, with no one to tell us the truth."

"That's not necessarily true. Our only real

lead is Robert. He was the last person to have seen Bruce alive. Even if he didn't see the killer there might have been something that he knew about Bruce, he may not even realize that it relates to Bruce's death."

"I think we should start in Bruce's office. Maybe he has something there about Dodge being released from prison. If he does we might be able to use it to highlight Dodge as a suspect." Jo shrugged. "Or maybe he knew more than he told me about the paintings, and there will be a clue that points directly at his killer."

"There is no way that you can break into his office." Eddy grimaced.

"Why not?"

"No way, Eddy's right, Jo. If you're caught breaking into his office there won't be any chance to keep you out of handcuffs. You have to stay clear of the gallery," Walt said.

"It has to be one of us, it can't be you, Jo," Eddy said.

"So, one of you is going to risk getting caught?"

"Maybe." Eddy rubbed his chin.

"Why don't I just get you in," Jo suggested.

"And then you'll disappear," Eddy said.

"Yes."

"That might work," Samantha said. "But it's risky."

"It will only take me a couple of minutes," Jo said. "I'm the best option for you to get in there."

"I don't like that idea," Walt said. "What if you get caught?"

"I won't, I studied the gallery's alarm system and lock when I was looking into the missing paintings for Bruce."

"Okay, I don't like it though." Walt stood up. "If we're going to do this, we'd better eat first. I don't want to have a nervous stomach."

"Maybe you should stay here with Jo when she comes back." Eddy nodded.

"Actually, if Walt is willing, he should go. His attention to detail is flawless. He might notice something that you and Samantha wouldn't," Jo said.

"Oh, good," Walt said, but he looked nervous.

"I'll drive Jo there in my car then we can come back here and try to find how connected David and Leela's lives were," Samantha said.

"Let's get something to eat before the games begin." Eddy wrung his hands.

They gathered at Samantha's house to review the case, share a meal, and plan what to look for in the office.

"Anything with Robert's name on it would be good. I want to know why Robert and Bruce met privately without David there. How much did Robert know about Bruce's suspicions of David?" Samantha tapped the notebook she'd drawn a chart on. "Robert might have tipped David off, and set the plan in motion to murder Bruce."

"That's possible." Eddy studied the flowing

handwriting on the paper. "When we spoke to him he acted as if he had nothing to say, but my instincts told me he was hiding something."

"We're going to find out what." Samantha smiled.

Eddy and Walt geared up for the search of the office, while Jo got everything ready to break in for them.

"Be careful, both of you. You don't want to have to face the consequences if you're caught." Jo looked between them. "And thank you."

"Don't worry, Jo, we've got this." Eddy winked at her. Walt patted her shoulder, then they left the villa.

"I'll see you there." Jo and Samantha followed after them in Samantha's car.

Chapter Seventeen

"Hurry up, Jo." Walt frowned as he stood in the shadow cast by the overhang of the gallery roof. "We're going to get spotted out here."

"Don't worry. I never fail." Jo smiled as she walked up to the back door of the gallery. She looked up and down the street as she fiddled with the lock. Within mere seconds the door clicked open. She walked in and pressed a few buttons on the alarm control panel. "It's disabled."

"Good work, Jo," Walt said with a hint of admiration.

"We'll see you at Samantha's," Eddy said sternly.

"But..." Jo started to protest.

"No arguments," Eddy said. Jo's shoulders slumped as she turned away.

"We're in, Walt, let's make this quick and clean." Eddy gestured to Walt in the shadows beside the gallery.

"Sh, Eddy." Walt frowned as he hurried past him into the gallery. Eddy rolled his eyes and followed after him. Once inside Eddy was careful not to touch anything.

"Look with your eyes, Walt, not with your hands, if you can help it."

"I can assure you I don't want to touch anything that I don't need to. I think we should start in the office. If there was any record of Dodge threatening Bruce it would be there."

"Good idea, the gallery is mostly paintings. The computer will probably still be gone for processing so we'll have to hope that Bruce kept some kind of hard copy records that the police might have overlooked." Eddy pulled his sleeve down over his hand and turned the knob on the office door. He pushed it open and stepped inside. The office was spacious enough for both of them to look around together. Walt began to sort through the desk, while Eddy checked behind paintings to see if there might have been a safe that was overlooked.

"There's nothing." Eddy shook his head. "The police have picked this place clean. Whatever we hoped to find, isn't here." He turned at the sound of a click.

"I think you're wrong about that, Eddy. Bruce knew his way around hiding places. There's a secret drawer in here." Walt tugged at something underneath the desk. Eddy walked over to take a look. Walt slid a long thin drawer out from beneath the desk and set it carefully on top. It was filled with papers and a leather bound book.

"It looks like the police might have missed something after all." He held up the book for Eddy to see.

"What's in the book?" Eddy peered over Walt's shoulder to have a closer look. Walt flipped the cover of the book open and scanned the handwritten text inside.

"It looks like a record of all of the paintings in

the gallery. There's a photograph of each of the paintings at the time of purchase as well."

"Interesting."

"He kept good records. He's also noted the paintings that have gone missing with details and a photo of each."

"Let me take some pictures of this, we can't take the book, but we can create our own on my phone." Eddy began to snap pictures of the paintings while Walt looked through the rest of the papers in the drawer.

"I don't see anything about Dodge in here, but there is this." He held up a slip of paper. "It looks like it was torn out of a date book. From what I can tell Bruce had an appointment with Robert Plathe, the day before he was killed. Before the meeting at the gallery."

"If they had a meeting scheduled the night Bruce died, then I wonder why Bruce was meeting with Robert the day before?"

"I'm not sure, but Robert will know. We need

to have another conversation with him."

"Here, let me get a picture of that, too." Eddy snapped a picture with his phone. "Anything else of interest in those papers?"

"I don't think so, but let's get as many pictures as we can."

"Then we have to get out of here as quickly as possible. David could come to the gallery at any moment."

"I can't believe they cleared him considering that he was having an affair with his partner's wife."

"At least, we think he was." Eddy pursed his lips. "It's easy to make assumptions."

After they finished documenting every record in the hidden drawer Eddy replaced the drawer. Then he sent a text to Chris to let him know about the hidden drawer. Hopefully, he wouldn't ask too many questions. Then the two slipped out as quickly as they had entered the gallery. When they returned to Samantha's villa, they shared the information they had found.

"Robert again, hmm?" Jo frowned. "He seems to have been more involved with Bruce than he's admitted."

"Oh, boys, I think we have a problem with our affair theory." Samantha held up a piece of paper that she had printed out. "Even though David has been to many of the same places that Leela has, I spoke to some of the waitresses and they were never there together. They were sometimes there on the same days, but they never dined together."

"So, you think it's all a coincidence?" Eddy narrowed his eyes.

"No, I don't, but I think we don't have any evidence that can prove that David was seeing Leela, which means we still have nothing to turn into the police."

"That's it." Jo stood up from the couch. "I think it's time I have a face to face conversation with Robert."

"Do you think that's wise, Jo? Again it puts

you in the middle of an investigation that you are the prime suspect in and you should be staying out of." Eddy quirked a brow. "When I spoke with him, he wasn't very interested in finding the killer."

"It'll just be a friendly chat. I don't know Robert, he doesn't know me, and we can have a conversation about what happened without me accusing him of anything. Besides, I'll take Walt." She smiled and grasped his shoulder.

"Me? Why?" Walt frowned.

"You'll notice if anything is off in Robert's gallery. Plus, you're great at spotting a lie."

"I guess I am pretty good at that." He smiled a little.

"Then it's settled, Jo and Walt will talk to Robert. I'll look into him more from here, and Eddy you need to check in with Chris about whether there is something the police know about the stolen paintings," Samantha said.

"Yes, I already tipped him off about the

hidden drawer we found. Hopefully the police won't figure out that someone else found it first. I haven't heard back from him yet, so I'll give him a call. You two make sure you're careful. We don't know how Robert is involved in all of this yet, but he could be connected with Dodge, or even David for that matter, so make the conversation light and don't back him into a corner." He locked eyes with Jo. "Got it?"

"Yes, I'll be as gentle as a feather."

"Ha." Eddy winked at her. "If you say so." He glanced at his watch. "The place might not even still be open."

"It's worth a shot. A lot of galleries stay open late on the weekends."

"I'll call you if I find anything of interest about Robert." Samantha sat down at her computer and began to type.

"All right, I guess it's you and me, Jo." Walt offered her his arm.

"I guess it is." She wrapped her arm around

his. As they left Samantha's villa Jo led Walt to her car. For once he didn't complain about the state of it, though she did spend more time cleaning it since meeting Walt. He was quiet as she drove towards Robert's gallery. When they were about five minutes away she looked over at him.

"Are you sure you're up for this, Walt? You don't have to do this if you don't want to."

"I'm sure."

"You seem nervous."

"I'm just regulating my heartbeat and temperature to prevent any indication that I'm lying."

"Seriously?" She looked over at him.

"Yes, it's quite easy to do really. With the right pace of breath and deep focus on a single calming image I can put myself in a near-meditative state."

"I thought you weren't into spiritual things?"

"There's nothing spiritual about meditation." He quirked a brow.

"There's not?" She laughed. "You could have fooled me. When I'm in yoga class it seems very spiritual to me."

"I can see why it would seem that way, as when the body is calm and relaxed it can create a sense of euphoria that could be confused with a spiritual experience." He shrugged and looked back through the windshield. "Whether you believe it's connecting you with the universe, or understand the scientific mechanics of meditation, it benefits the body and the brain so there is no risk involved. I don't mean to belittle any spiritual experience that you've had, I am in no place to say that it wasn't genuine. I just personally have not experienced it for myself, and have no interest in that use of meditation."

"Maybe you just haven't done it right." She smiled as he looked over at her.

"Maybe I haven't. You'll have to show me your version some time."

"I'd love to." She parked a short distance from

the gallery and watched the door for a moment. "Let's give it a minute to be sure there's no one else in the gallery. Having company could complicate things."

"Good plan." Walt sat back against the seat and closed his eyes. He continued to regulate his breathing. Jo's focus was on the front door as it opened. She gasped when she saw the person who walked out with Robert. She grabbed for her binoculars so fast that Walt jumped in reaction to the sudden movement. Jo put the binoculars to her eyes and watched the two at the front door. She was able to confirm that the woman she looked at was Bruce's wife, Leela. As she watched, Robert wrapped his arms around her and planted a heavy kiss on her lips. Jo dropped the binoculars.

"Jo, what is it?" Walt reached to the floorboard to pick up the binoculars, by the time he started to sit back up, Jo's hand was on his back with the strength to force him back down.

"Stay down. I know that woman. That's

Bruce's wife. I don't want her to know that I saw her."

"Okay." Walt looked into her eyes as they hunched close together. "Do you think she had something to do with Bruce's death?"

"I didn't before, but now I think she might have. She's clearly having an affair."

"Bruce is dead, Jo, she's a widow. She can kiss whoever she likes."

"Oh believe me, Walt, this isn't the first time they've kissed."

"You've seen them together before?" His brows knitted.

"No, but you don't kiss a man that you just met like that."

"You don't?" His voice softened some.

"No."

"How do you kiss a man you just met?"

Jo's cheeks flushed and she looked away from him as best as she could in the tight space. "With a lot less passion."

"Oh, I see." He smiled and blushed slightly. "Shall I take a look and see if they're done?"

"Yes please. But don't get spotted."

Walt eased his head up some, then dipped back down so fast that his lips brushed across Jo's forehead.

"They're gone. Bruce just went back inside and Leela is walking away. Sorry about that. Let me get a wipe."

Jo sat up slowly. "Don't worry, Walt, I'm not afraid of your lips."

Walt opened his mouth to respond, but she was already out the door. He followed after her until she reached the gallery door.

"Jo wait." He caught her hand with his. "Are you sure you're in the right state for this?"

"I'm fine." She smiled at him and gave his hand a squeeze. "You regulate your breathing, I'm just really good at lying." She winked at him then held the door open for him. Walt stepped through, then Jo followed after. Robert looked up from a desk in the front of the gallery and smiled at them.

"Welcome. Is there anything in particular that you're interested in?"

"Something for over the mantle." Walt nodded towards Jo. "It needs to suit her taste."

"Ah, I see. You must be the one with the eye for detail?"

"You could say that." She locked eyes with Robert. "I want something that will represent loyalty in a relationship. Something that says, this is for life."

"Oh, I understand your meaning." He nodded. "I have a few that might fit that request. Let's take a walk around the gallery." As he led her through the paintings it took everything inside of Jo to keep her from confronting him about his relationship with Leela. She had assumed the woman was a grieving widow when she helped pack up the house for her. Now she believed differently.

As they walked Walt skimmed through the pictures on his phone of the list of paintings that were stolen from Bruce's gallery. He didn't notice any of the paintings, however one did catch his attention.

"Can you tell me about this painting?" Walt pointed to it.

"Oh sure, it's a Randalph, quite expensive. What is your budget?"

"This Randalph, is it one of a kind?"

"Of course."

"You're sure?"

"Yes." He laughed. "I only sell one of a kind paintings here. It is fully authenticated and ready to hang on your wall. What do you think, miss?" He looked over at Jo. Jo paused in front of the painting. She wasn't sure why Walt was so interested in it, but whatever the reason she wanted to play along.

"It's a bit blue."

"Yes, Randalph was known for his blues. Would it clash with the décor of your living room?"

"I'm afraid it might. What do you think, love?" She tilted her head towards Walt.

"Let's take a picture of it, so we can decide how it looks at home." He pulled out his phone and took a picture of the painting. "I think we should discuss this a bit more before we make a purchase. Thank you for your time. We'll be in touch."

"No problem. Buying a painting of this value is a big decision and it is always best to be certain that it is something you want in your living room. Let me walk you out." He followed them towards the door.

Jo shot a glance over at Walt. She could tell that he had something on his mind. As soon as they were in the car she looked at him.

"Spill. What did you figure out?"

"He's a crook. A criminal of the worst kind. A forger."

"What do you mean?"

"Look at this." He pointed to the picture of the painting on his phone. "I took it because it's the exact same painting that is currently hanging on the wall in Bruce's gallery."

"What? But that's impossible." She looked at the painting in the photograph. "Wow, it does look the same from what I can remember."

"Look at this." Walt brought up the picture of the painting in Bruce's gallery that was featured on the gallery website, and placed the two photographs side by side on his phone. "Do you see anything different?"

She searched the paintings for any subtle differences then shook her head. "Nothing."

"Except for this." Walt tapped the bottom right corner of each picture. "The signatures are just a little different. When I am trying to spot a forgery I always look at the signature, because it is one of the hardest things to fake. The letter R in this signature is boxy and wide, while in this signature it's curvy and tight. There is no way that the same person signed these paintings."

"But how do we know which one is the fake?"

"Robert said his painting was fully authenticated. Maybe Bruce was forging paintings. Maybe that's why he and Robert really met, because Robert figured it out."

"Or it could have been the other way around. Maybe Robert was lying about them being authenticated and he was forging paintings and Bruce found out."

"That's possible, it makes more sense. If Bruce accused him of selling forgeries that would give Robert motive to kill Bruce."

"Yes, it would. We need to get in there and find out for certain. If Robert gets nervous he might hide or destroy any evidence."

"We should go back to the others first and update them on what we found."

"No. I need to do this now, Walt. Robert is going to run if he senses the slightest suspicion. If he's with Leela and she's cleaning out her house as fast as she is then they have an escape planned. I'm going in there."

"But Robert is in there."

"So we'll draw him out."

"Jo. Let's regroup and make a plan."

"All right, all right." She sighed.

Chapter Eighteen

As the four friends gathered around the table in Samantha's villa yet again, the discussion became heated.

"I'm sure that Robert had something to do with this. He wanted Leela, and he needed to get rid of Bruce to have her," Jo said.

"The only thing we really have is the fact that it looks like he was having an affair and he is possibly forging paintings." Samantha shook her head. "That doesn't make him a murderer."

"No, we have more than that. He was there around the time of the murder," Jo said.

"But the cameras didn't catch him." Eddy tapped the table.

"Because they were disabled," Samantha added.

"And only David and Bruce had the password." Walt sighed. "So how did he do it?"

"He didn't need the password, he had Leela. Think about it. Don't most husbands and wives trust each other enough to share passwords? Maybe Bruce asked Leela to do some work on the computer and gave it to her? So she gave it to Robert. Robert met with Bruce at the gallery, showed his face on camera entering and leaving, then slipped back in with a key Leela gave him, and disabled the cameras so that he could murder Bruce."

"Wait, he told me the police cleared him, he was at the restaurant with his girlfriend."

"His girlfriend provided him an alibi. Maybe it was even Leela. He met her there before going to the gallery so the staff could see him, then killed Bruce, and returned. Restaurants are too busy to keep track of every patron. The receipt shows he paid, and the waiter said he was there because he saw him. But I'm sure he didn't pay attention to the exact time. It could easily have been Robert."

"She's right." Walt shook his head. "It's not much of an alibi, with the restaurant being so close."

"Okay, let's say he did do it. Why? So, he was seeing Leela, he didn't have to kill Bruce." Eddy rested his hands on the table. "What was his motivation?"

"Maybe it wasn't David stealing the paintings at all. Maybe Bruce discovered that Robert was making forgeries of the missing paintings and other paintings. Robert could have been stealing them, to copy them, then sell the original on the black market and still make a profit from the copy." Walt nodded. "It would probably take some time before people realized that the painting hanging in his gallery was reported stolen, especially since Bruce was convinced that David was the thief."

"Okay, so we think that Robert killed Bruce. But we still don't have proof." Eddy glanced around the table at his friends. "How are we going to get it?"

"I'm going to get it." Jo straightened up. "I'm

going tonight, to get it. I'm not letting him get away with this. Leela is planning to run, and from the way they were kissing I'm betting that she's planning to take Robert with her. If we wait any longer, the evidence will be gone."

"I don't know, maybe we should think this through a little more." Eddy sat down at the table. "Let's plan it for tomorrow night."

"No. I'm sorry, Eddy, but I'm not asking for permission. I'm going tonight, and Walt is coming with me."

"What?" Walt gulped.

"I should go instead of you." Eddy stood up again.

"Not this time, Eddy. I need to do this. It was my friend that was murdered. I know how to steal paintings, Walt knows how to spot a forgery. We will be fine."

Eddy opened his mouth to protest, then closed it. "All right. If that's what you think is best, then go for it."

"Thanks Eddy." Jo smiled.

***

Ten minutes later Jo was in the passenger seat of Walt's car. She bit her tongue as he crawled along the highway. Cars zoomed past them, the drivers offered colorful gestures. Walt didn't seem to notice. He rode the speed limit on the dot, and never took his eyes from the road. After what felt like an eternity they parked at Robert's gallery.

"His car isn't here. I think we're safe."

"Safe? Breaking into the gallery of a killer is safe?" Walt stared at her with wide eyes.

"We're going to be just fine, Walt. All we have to do is get one of the forged paintings. If we can find one, that should be enough proof to take to Detective Rowan and get the attention off me."

"I think we should have brought Eddy along." Walt frowned.

"Eddy didn't want us to do this, and you are the only one with a good enough eye for detail to figure out which paintings are fake." She gave his hand a slight tug as they approached the gallery. "Don't you want to see my skills?"

"Uh, well I uh." He frowned as she neared the back door. "Don't you think there's an alarm."

"I'm certain there is one, which is a very good thing. Did you know that alarms actually make it easier to break in?"

"That's not possible." Walt shook his head.

"It is, because once you know the weakness of every alarm system, they become useless. But even if someone catches a glimpse of a strange figure going inside a building, they won't pay attention to it because the alarm isn't going off. It's the main line of defense, and all it takes is disconnecting it to get inside. It's as simple as flipping a light switch."

"I doubt it's that simple."

"Okay, maybe not that simple, especially these newer systems, but simple enough that it can be done. My point is the alarm systems give people a false sense of security and that's when they get sloppy. They don't always lock up correctly, or stow away valuables."

Jo popped open a small, metal door not far from the back door. Inside was an assortment of switches.

"If you disconnect the alarm won't it send a signal to the alarm company and the police?"

"If you were to cut the wire, sure. Or if you were to enter the wrong code, absolutely. But not if you cut the phone lines and power to the entire building. By doing that, the alarm system has no ability to transmit a signal anywhere." She began to toy with the switches until she found the one she wanted. "The key is in which system you shut down first." She threw the switch, then followed up with several others. The few lights that glowed inside the gallery shut off as did the eerie glow of the alarm panel just inside the door. She then proceeded to the lock and opened it with just a few movements of one of her tools.

"See? Without an alarm system Robert

probably would have installed a lot more locks in order to prevent someone from getting in. Instead he put in a cheap lock that is one of the easiest to pick."

"Maybe he thought that he would catch anyone who attempted to break in because the alarm system would announce the entry."

"Probably." Jo shrugged. "But no matter what the reason, we're in. Shall we?"

"You really do have skills." Walt smiled as he studied her for a moment. "I hope you're as good at escaping as you are at breaking in."

"Me too." She grinned and grabbed his hand. "Let's go." She led him through the dark interior of the gallery. Walt fumbled for his flashlight, but she grabbed his arm before he could pull it out of his pocket. "No flashlights."

"How are we going to know where to go?"

"Just stick with me, I memorized the floorplan." She kept one hand wrapped around his as they weaved deeper into the gallery.

"No wait, this way." Walt sniffed the air.

"Why?" She glanced over her shoulder at him.

"I can smell it."

"Smell what?"

"Wet paint. Someone's been painting in here. None of the paintings should have that fresh scent of paint."

"Okay, tell me if I'm going in the wrong direction." Together they moved through the gallery.

"Here." Walt tugged at her hand. "This is it."

Jo stared at the empty wall where they stopped. She wasn't sure what to think. The wall didn't have a single painting hung on it, and its surface was dry. She brushed her gloved fingertips along it to be sure, then the wall itself moved. She shuddered as she realized there was a hidden door. As it swung open she noticed a glowing light and the scuff of shoes.

"Walt, run!" She started to shove him away,

but it was too late. Robert grabbed Walt hard by the shoulder and shoved him inside the room. In the next breath Jo was on her knees beside the spot where Walt collapsed.

"Couldn't stay away, could you?" Robert chuckled and kicked the door shut. "Don't worry, it's soundproof in here. No one is going to hear you cry for help." He reached into his pocket, pulled a gun out and pointed it at them.

"How could you do this, Robert? It's one thing to steal paintings and forge paintings, it's another thing to murder someone," Jo said.

"It was not my original plan. My original plan was to include Bruce in my activities. I wanted his experience and his expertise. I even tried to turn him against his partner so he'd be more interested in a partnership with me. However, the more time I spent with him the more I understood that he would never be involved in anything criminal again. How anyone can think paying huge amounts of money for a silly little painting isn't criminal, is beyond me. Once I recognized that I decided to leave him alone."

"But not his wife?"

"Ah, so you noticed that?"

"It was rather hard not to." Jo narrowed her eyes. "Does she know that you murdered her husband?"

"Does she know?" He laughed.

"No, I didn't know." Jo jumped at the sound of the voice. She turned towards it and saw Leela with her hands tied together lying on the floor in the corner. Jo noticed a bruise on her head as she slowly sat up. Her cheeks were streaked with mascara.

"Oh you're awake, darling." Robert laughed, but his eyes were as cold as steel. "She's the one who gave me the idea, although she never realized it until now. Bruce had discovered that several of my paintings were forgeries and was going to prove this at our meeting at his gallery. He even offered to help me through the legal system if I would turn myself in. A valiant man to the end.

Too bad for him, I have no interest in going to prison. Too bad for you as well." He kept the gun pointed between the three of them.

"I never told you to kill him," Leela said with desperation. "I just wanted to be with you."

"Ah please, you didn't want me, you just wanted more excitement in your life." Robert laughed.

"I just wanted to have some fun. I didn't want you to kill him."

"So stealing is okay but murder isn't?" Robert looked at Leela.

"We were just meant to get some money from the paintings and have a little fun. Get some money. Not murder!" Leela cried out.

"Ugh, it was a means to an end." Robert laughed. "We had some fun, now I need to move on and tie up some loose ends."

"Loose ends?" Leela scowled.

"I'll be going now. Unfortunately, you're not

going to be able to join me." As he moved around them towards the door of the hidden room Jo noticed that a key dangled from his pocket. She also detected the strong scent of paint thinners and paints that filled the room. When he pulled the key from his pocket she saw the lighter attached.

"Walt! He's going to set the place on fire!"

"What?" Walt gasped.

"She's right. Smart as a whip this one. What a waste." He flicked the lighter on and stepped through the door.

"Don't leave me," Leela cried. "You can't do this!"

"Sorry darling, business is business."

"Business?"

"It will be a tragedy in the newspaper tomorrow. A gallery burned to the foundation, all of that beautiful art gone forever. I'll get the insurance money and it will make the value of the paintings I've stashed away in the fireproof safe skyrocket. Now, I can kill two birds with one stone, so to speak. Good timing. Good night friends." He flicked the lighter on and waved the flame close to a pile of papers on a desk beside the door. Before the flame could ignite anything the flame was extinguished.

"They are not your friends." Eddy's sharp voice carried through the room just before Robert was jerked out through the door. Jo sprang forward and helped Eddy tackle Robert to the ground. Samantha poked her head into the room.

"Come on out, Walt, it's safe."

Walt made his way slowly through the door and into the hallway. "Just in time, Eddy."

"Actually we were here for a few minutes, but we had to get the confession of course."

"I do hope you're joking." Walt stared at him. "He was waving a lighter around in there."

"I know, I blew it out." Eddy laughed. "Don't worry, Walt, I wasn't going to let him start the fire. I just wanted to have a little bit of fun."

"Your version of fun is very twisted."

"Maybe so, but it's all I have, one of life's small pleasures. Everyone is okay, right? Well, other than Robert." He looked down at the man beneath his shoe. "Detective Rowan will be along shortly to take care of him."

"I don't understand why you and Samantha even came here. I'm glad you did, don't get me wrong, but why?" Jo shifted her gaze between them.

"Actually, you have David to thank for that," Samantha said.

"David?" Jo's eyes widened. "Why?"

"He stopped by your villa. When we spotted him we thought he was there to harm you, so we confronted him. Instead he said he was there to warn you. Remember all of the transactions he made at expensive restaurants and women's clothing stores?" Samantha asked.

"Yes." Jo frowned. "What does that have to do with anything?"

"Apparently he'd been tracking Leela. He was out on a date one night and noticed Leela and Robert at the same restaurant," Samantha explained. "He grew suspicious and began to follow her. He suspected that Leela and Robert were having an affair. When Bruce turned up dead, he suspected that Robert and Leela were involved, but he didn't have proof, and didn't want to put himself in the middle of things. But he started to worry that things might get out of control if he didn't say something. He came to your villa to warn you about Robert, because he knew how much Bruce cared about you."

"Which reminded me, just how much I care about you." Eddy shrugged. "So I decided to stop being a modern man and get over here to make sure that you were safe."

"And for once, I agreed with him." Samantha smiled. "When we heard Robert talking I started recording his confession." Samantha held up her phone. "He won't be charming his way out of this one."

"I'm sorry, Jo," Leela said shakily as she still sat on the floor.

"Did you steal the paintings?" Jo scowled at Leela.

"No, not myself."

"But you helped him?" Jo asked.

"I gave Robert the alarm details and passwords to steal the paintings."

"Bruce was killed because you were greedy, you wanted money." Jo stared at her.

"It wasn't that. I was just so bored and he brought some excitement to my life."

"But Bruce was murdered."

"I know, I would have said something, but I didn't think Robert could do this," Leela said. "I thought Robert cared about me."

"You gave him an alibi?" Eddy asked.

"No, I didn't, he met with someone else, an ex-girlfriend. at the restaurant and she gave him an alibi."

"But you knew he went to the gallery on the day that Bruce was murdered," Eddy said.

"I did," Leela said. "But he said that when he got to the gallery to steal the paintings the police were already there. Bruce was already dead."

"And you believed me," Robert said from beneath Eddy's shoe. "It was all your fault, you are so gullible. I didn't want you. I just wanted the money."

Jo stared down at the man on the floor. The man who planned to leave her and Walt in a burning room.

"Bruce was an honorable man," Jo said. "He gave you one last chance to come clean and instead you took his life from him. Whatever the courts do to you will be far less than you deserve."

"He was a thief, just like you are. Once a criminal, always a criminal." He glared up at her from the floor.

Eddy applied a little more pressure to his back with his heavy boot. "The criminal is the one I'm standing on." He looked up at Jo. "If you want to leave before the police arrive, I'll understand."

"No." She folded her arms across her chest and smiled. "I'm staying right here. I want to see Detective Rowan's face when I hand him his murderer."

Chapter Nineteen

The next day at sunrise, Jo walked to the edge of the lake again. As happy as she was that Bruce's killer was found, she still felt like she needed to say good-bye to an old friend, a man who had saved her life. She slipped out of her shoes and stuck her toes into the water. In her hands she clasped a bouquet of flowers. As the sky transformed with the first rays of dawn, her heart swelled with memories of Bruce. She felt that by finding his murderer she had finally repaid him for saving her life. For the first time she could look back at the person she was, without a sense of loathing or regret. She was a good person then, too, just as Bruce was.

"Goodbye Bruce. Thank you, for your kindness, and your bravery."

"Thank you, Bruce." Samantha slipped her arm through Jo's. "For taking care of Jo."

Jo looked over at her with surprise and

noticed Eddy and Walt behind her. "You're all here."

"We are." Walt stepped up on the other side of her and Eddy stood next to him.

Jo released the flowers into the water. "Because of him I had a chance at a new life. I thought what mattered most was my freedom, which of course is important. But now I know, what mattered more than that was having someone who offered his loyalty. I valued it then, and thanks to all of you, now I value it even more."

"You're stuck with us, kid." Eddy smiled.

"Absolutely." Samantha nudged her side.

"As long as you'll have us." Walt met her eyes and held them for a long moment.

"Thank you." Jo smiled at them. She no longer felt as if she had two lives, but one long winding one, a journey that traversed the most difficult times, and led her to the sweetest reward. Maybe there were still sunsets to come, but she was certain that the memory of that day's sunrise would be all she needed to make it through the rest of her journey.

The End

More Cozy Mysteries by Cindy Bell

Sage Gardens Cozy Mysteries

Birthdays Can Be Deadly

Money Can Be Deadly

Trust Can Be Deadly

Ties Can Be Deadly

Rocks Can Be Deadly

Numbers Can Be Deadly

Nuts about Nuts Cozy Mysteries

A Tough Case to Crack

Chocolate Centered Cozy Mysteries

The Sweet Smell of Murder

A Deadly Delicious Delivery

A Bitter Sweet Murder

A Treacherous Tasty Trail

Luscious Pastry at a Lethal Party

Trouble and Treats

Dune House Cozy Mysteries

Seaside Secrets

Boats and Bad Guys

Treasured History

Hidden Hideaways

Dodgy Dealings

Suspects and Surprises

Heavenly Highland Inn Cozy Mysteries

Murdering the Roses

Dead in the Daisies

Killing the Carnations

Drowning the Daffodils

Suffocating the Sunflowers

Books, Bullets and Blooms

A Deadly serious Gardening Contest

A Bridal Bouquet and a Body

Wendy the Wedding Planner Cozy Mysteries

Matrimony, Money and Murder

Chefs, Ceremonies and Crimes

Knives and Nuptials

Mice, Marriage and Murder

Bekki the Beautician Cozy Mysteries

Hairspray and Homicide

A Dyed Blonde and a Dead Body

Mascara and Murder

Pageant and Poison

Conditioner and a Corpse

Mistletoe, Makeup and Murder

Hairpin, Hair Dryer and Homicide

Blush, a Bride and a Body

Shampoo and a Stiff

Cosmetics, a Cruise and a Killer

Lipstick, a Long Iron and Lifeless

Camping, Concealer and Criminals

Treated and Dyed